D0753763

Jean Rhys was born in Dominica in 1890, the daughter of a Welsh doctor and a white Creole mother. When she was sixteen she came to England where, after her father died, she drifted into a series of jobs, including chorus girl, mannequin and artist's model.

She began to write while in her thirties and living in Paris following the break-up of the first of her three marriages. Her first book was published in 1927, a collection of stories called *The Left Bank*. This was followed by *Quartet* (originally published as *Postures*, 1928), *After Leaving Mr Mackenzie* (1930), *Voyage in the Dark* (1934) and *Good Morning, Midnight* (1939). With the outbreak of the Second World War and the failure of *Good Morning, Midnight*, the books went out of print, and Jean Rhys disappeared from the literary scene. It was generally thought that she was dead.

Many years later she was rediscovered, living reclusively in Cornwall. During the missing years, she had accumulated the stories collected in *Tigers are Better-Looking*. In 1966 she made a sensational reappearance with *Wide Sargasso Sea*, which won the Royal Society of Literature Award and the W. H. Smith Award for that year. Her only comment on her sudden great success was 'It has come too late.' Her final collection of stories, *Sleep It Off Lady*, appeared in 1976. She was made a Fellow of the Royal Society of Literature in 1966 and a CBE in 1978. *Smile Please*, her unfinished autobiography, was published after her death in 1979.

Hilary Jenkins studied English Literature at Oxford University and completed her M.Litt. on the history of children's literature. She has taught Literature and English as a Foreign Language in Oxford, India, China and Saudi Arabia. She joined the British Council in 1988 and since 1996 has been Literature Education Manager, with responsibility for the annual Oxford Conference on the Teaching of Literature Overseas, and editor of *Literature Matters*.

Ronald Carter is Professor of Modern English Language in the School of English Studies, University of Nottingham. He has published widely in the field of language and literature studies and applied linguistics and English teaching. He is the co-author with John McRae of *The Penguin Guide to English Literature* (1996) and *The Routledge History of Literature in English: Britain and Ireland* (1997).

John McRae is Special Professor of Language in Literature Studies in the School of English Studies at the University of Nottingham. He is the author or editor of more than forty books, including, with Ronald Carter, *The Penguin Guide to English Literature*. He has lectured in over forty countries worldwide.

Penguin Student Editions
Series editors: Ronald Carter and John McRae

Other titles in this series:

Jean Rhys

sea without shores in a sense

Wide Sargasso Sea

because of seaweed

in the Atlantic ocean
> body of water within a body of water

Edited by Hilary Jenkins

has no currents within it. stagnant

"Nature is as indifferent as God. Its beauty contrasts with, heightens, and makes more unfortunate human cruelty and folly."

"looking back" — Antoinette realizes journies cannot be unmade; so she tries to understand the paths taken by her mother and herself. Paradoxically, madness is the beginning of her voyage to truth and understanding.

PENGUIN BOOKS

PENGUIN BOOKS

Published by the Penguin Group
Penguin Books Ltd, 80 Strand, London WC2R 0RL, England
Penguin Putnam Inc., 375 Hudson Street, New York, New York 10014, USA
Penguin Books Australia Ltd, 250 Camberwell Road, Camberwell, Victoria 3124, Australia
Penguin Books Canada Ltd, 10 Alcorn Avenue, Toronto, Ontario, Canada M4V 3B2
Penguin Books India (P) Ltd, 11 Community Centre, Panchsheel Park, New Delhi – 110 017, India
Penguin Books (NZ) Ltd, Cnr Rosedale and Airborne Roads, Albany, Auckland, New Zealand
Penguin Books (South Africa) (Pty) Ltd, 24 Sturdee Avenue, Rosebank 2196, South Africa

Penguin Books Ltd, Registered Offices: 80 Strand, London WC2R 0RL, England

www.penguin.com

First published by André Deutsch 1966
Published in Penguin Books 1968
Published in Penguin Student Editions 2001

19

Set in 9.75/12.5 pt PostScript Monotype Plantin
Typeset by Rowland Phototypesetting Ltd, Bury St Edmunds, Suffolk
Printed in England by Clays Ltd, St Ives plc

ISBN-13: 978–0–140–81803–1

www.greenpenguin.co.uk

Penguin Books is committed to a sustainable future
for our business, our readers and our planet.
The book in your hands is made from paper
certified by the Forest Stewardship Council.

Contents

Introduction

Wide Sargasso Sea is a highly dramatic story, exotic, psychological, feminine and mysterious. It was published in 1966 when the author Jean Rhys was 76, and some 27 years after her previous novel.

It is the story of Antoinette Cosway, a white girl who grows up in the Caribbean, has a disastrous arranged marriage, and goes mad, imprisoned in an English country house.

It is also the previously untold story of Bertha Mason, the first Mrs Rochester in Charlotte Brontë's *Jane Eyre* (1847), although she is given a different name. *Wide Sargasso Sea* sets out to answer the question of why Bertha Mason/Antoinette Cosway might have gone mad in the first place.

Wide Sargasso Sea uses *Jane Eyre* as an imaginative starting-point. But the point of view is changed from the first-person narrative of Jane to that of Bertha Mason/Antoinette Cosway. *Wide Sargasso Sea* is therefore a rewriting of the classic text from the point of view of the most marginalized character in Brontë's novel: Bertha Mason is not only mad and female, the imprisoned, rejected wife, but also she comes from Jamaica, one of Britain's colonies.

Jean Rhys read *Jane Eyre* soon after publishing her second novel in 1939, and she worked on her response to it for many years before finally publishing in 1966. She gave it several different titles over the years. In a letter of 1949, Jean Rhys calls the book 'The first Mrs Rochester', and adds 'profound apologies to Charlotte Brontë and a deep curtsey too' (*Jean Rhys: Letters 1931–1966*, ed. Francis Wyndham and Diana Melly (Harmondsworth: Penguin, 1985, p. 64)). She liked and respected both Charlotte Brontë and *Jane Eyre*, but she felt the story was incomplete. It took her a long time to work out exactly what she wanted to say, and at times she thought she couldn't do it. In that same letter she said: 'It really haunts me that I can't finish it though.'

But although it takes *Jane Eyre* as its inspiration, *Wide Sargasso Sea* is set in time before that novel. Charlotte Brontë tells us that Bertha Mason is older than Jane Eyre, and five years older even than Mr Rochester. In fact Jean Rhys altered the possible dates of the narrative in *Jane Eyre* (where the action covers the 1820s and 30s) to suit her own story. She starts the action of *Wide Sargasso Sea* soon after 1833, an important date for the colonies because that was when the Emancipation Act banning slavery was passed. Later at school Antoinette embroiders the date 1839, and soon after this she is married and taken to England. *Wide Sargasso Sea* is a kind of prequel to *Jane Eyre*, because it describes the childhood of Bertha Mason and the early days of her marriage, which are not described in Charlotte Brontë's novel. But it also does more than this. As Alexis Lykiard says in his memoir of Jean Rhys, her 'original achievement in *Wide Sargasso Sea* was to extend, explore and modernize, while also rendering timeless, that cry, that yearning, and all those other vital elements she rediscovered in Brontë's novel' (*Jean Rhys Revisited*, Alexis Lykiard (Exeter: Stride, 2000, p. 88).

This form of 'rewriting' classic texts, questioning their assumptions, is part of the phenomenon often called 'writing back'. Texts like Shakespeare's *The Tempest* and Defoe's *Robinson Crusoe* have given modern writers the opportunity to bring a new perception to bear on familiar stories. Whether this is to be called 'post-colonial' is a question of debate, but it certainly reflects the presence of new voices 'writing back' to the traditions of classic English literature.

Jean Rhys said in a letter that when she read about Bertha Mason in *Jane Eyre* she thought: 'That's only one side – the English side' (*Letters*, p. 297). She expanded this in an interview:

The mad first wife in *Jane Eyre* has always interested me. I was convinced Charlotte Brontë must have had something against the West Indies and I was angry about it. Otherwise why did she take a West Indian for the horrible lunatic, for that really dreadful creature? (quoted by Hannah Carter, 'Fated to be Sad', *The Guardian*, 8 August 1968, p. 5).

Herself born in Dominica, in the West Indies, Jean Rhys was annoyed to find that Charlotte Brontë had made the first Mrs Rochester, a white Creole like herself, into a monster. Part of her reason for writing the book, therefore, was to expose what she saw as the latent racism at the heart of one of the great novels in the canon of English literature. Another reason was to examine its equally latent sexism: Charlotte Brontë allows Mr Rochester a second chance despite his many faults. The image of womanhood that Jane Eyre represents is set against Bertha's, and the first wife is found lacking and is set aside. Rhys questions the values of the earlier novel by rewriting the story of *Jane Eyre* from the point of view of the other woman, the rejected wife. This is why she gives her another name, Antoinette Cosway, and then traces her transformation into Bertha Mason.

Jean Rhys felt marginalized herself. She was an outsider, both as a woman and as a colonial. She was a person of colour, a person whose language was not 'standard' English. Just as her lifestyle was unconventional, so her novels handle unconventional themes in unconventional ways.

Why the title? The Sargasso Sea is an area of the Atlantic Ocean lying between Europe and the Caribbean, where ships were often becalmed. It was said to be full of weeds that would trap a ship, killing all those on board in the becalmed waters under the hot sun. It is an image of the no man's land between people and between cultures, full of fears, dreams and nightmares.

Jean Rhys's first idea for the title was 'Le Revenant', meaning the zombie or the one who comes back from the dead, and this title would have emphasized the sense of haunting and being haunted. The book is indeed full of ghosts and magic and 'revenant'-type experiences: the distinctions between reality and unreality, life and death, day and night, present and past, are continually blurred. What never changes is the sense of fear. Right at the beginning Antoinette says, 'My father, visitors, horses, feeling safe in bed – all belonged to the past' (p. 3), and the sense of foreboding, of fears imminent and realized, dominates the book.

Wide Sargasso Sea is told through the voices of Antoinette, Mr Rochester (though he is never named) and (briefly) Grace Poole (the servant in *Jane Eyre* who acts as Antoinette's jailer). It is about the failure of a marriage and the disastrous consequences for the woman, but it is also about the equally disastrous relationship between England and her colonies. It is in three parts: the first describes Antoinette's childhood, the second the failure of her marriage, and the last, much shorter, part reveals what might (or might not) happen.

In the first part we see how isolated Antoinette is. Her mother neglects her for her mentally handicapped brother. She has only one friend, Tia, who later steals her dress and throws stones at her. The only person she trusts is Christophine, her nanny, yet she is also afraid of her, because she practises obeah, or magic. But even Christophine's magic cannot save her from an unhappy marriage.

The second part is set after the wedding, and the story is taken over by the nameless man who we later learn is Mr Rochester. He changes Antoinette's name to Bertha, and the failure of their marriage is described from his point of view. Although to begin with he thinks Antoinette is beautiful, he becomes increasingly afraid of her and of the strange place where they spend their honeymoon. He does not like not being in control, and he starts to believe rumours about the madness of Antoinette's mother and brother, and about the sexual incontinence and incipient madness of Antoinette herself.

By the end of Part Two Antoinette has become a kind of slave; she has lost her happiness, her husband's love, her name, her money and her freedom. This loss reflects her role as a woman in the society of her day, but also the colonial system. Mr Rochester believes all the stories he is told about her mixed blood and loose morals. He is frightened by the place because it is not England, and he behaves just like the old slave owners. Although he does not want Antoinette to be his wife, he does not want her to go free either. He decides to keep her prisoner, and take her money.

In Part Three the action of the novel moves to England, and into the world of *Jane Eyre*. Antoinette/Bertha even talks about being inside cardboard covers. *Wide Sargasso Sea* ends with Antoinette/Bertha about to set the house on fire. We assume that she will kill herself, although we cannot know for sure whether that will happen. She simply says: 'Now at last I know why I was brought here and what I have to do' (p. 123).

It is not necessary to have read *Jane Eyre* in order to enjoy *Wide Sargasso Sea*, although most readers will know of it. Still, there are some interesting parallels and cross-references. Jean Rhys makes Antoinette Cosway and Jane Eyre quite similar. As children they both endure poverty, friendlessness and the isolation of boarding school. Later, however, Jane Eyre's value is recognized and she marries Mr Rochester, who was previously her employer. They live happily ever after, whereas poor Antoinette does not.

Of course there are several twists to the plot in Charlotte Brontë's novel, and these are where the reader can find the intersections with the later book. For example, Jane slowly becomes aware that there is something mysterious and concealed at Thornfield Hall. She hears strange noises. One night a fire is started in Mr Rochester's bedroom (from which Jane rescues him). A visitor, a Mr Mason, is attacked. The truth is revealed only when Rochester and Jane's wedding is interrupted by the revelation that there is a first Mrs Rochester, Bertha Antoinetta Mason, still living. Mr Rochester then tells Jane the story of how he was tricked into marrying a Creole heiress who turned out to be mad and whom he now keeps, locked up, on the third storey of the house.

When he takes Jane upstairs to show her how unsuitable a wife Bertha is for him, Jane realizes she has already seen Bertha in the night, tearing up Jane's wedding veil. She describes Bertha as having 'a discoloured face . . . a savage face' (*Jane Eyre* (Penguin Student Edition, 1999), p. 321) with 'fearful blackened inflation' of the features, 'the lips were swelled and dark'. Charlotte Brontë's description of Bertha appealed to contemporary racist prejudices, as well as sexual ones. She is described as unfit for Mr Rochester because she is 'intemperate and unchaste' (*Jane Eyre*, p. 349), and the implication is that her madness was caused by sexual excess: 'her excesses had prematurely developed the germs of insanity' (*Jane Eyre*, p. 350). She is also referred to as non-human, being called variously a demon, a witch, a vampire, a beast, a hyena and a goblin.

At the end of *Jane Eyre*, Bertha Mason sets fire to the house and kills herself. While trying to rescue her, Mr Rochester is injured and blinded. Later, Jane returns to marry him, but only when she has received her own fortune which, like Mr Rochester's money, also comes from the colonies. Her uncle in Madeira represented the same firm as Mr Mason in the West Indies.

Jean Rhys sets out to show in her novel how the first Mrs Rochester may have been driven to madness by the patriarchal and colonial systems, from which both Mr Rochester and Jane Eyre also get their money. Not surprisingly, she shows that there are clear connections between the two. As Penny Boumelha has pointed out, when Jean Rhys set out to vindicate 'the madwoman', she emphasized her role as 'the legacy of imperialism concealed in the heart of every English gentleman's castle'(Penny Boumelha, 'Jane Eyre, Jamaica and the Gentleman's House', *Southern Review*, 21, 2 (July 1988), p. 112).

In writing-back in this way, Jean Rhys is not simply filling in the gaps in the story to help us appreciate the Brontë text more. Instead she is changing how we see the classic novel. By giving voice to the marginalized and silenced (the mad woman, the colonized) she enables us to see the story of *Jane Eyre* in a context larger than that of England in the nineteenth century. Just as *Wide Sargasso Sea* is full of the ghosts of the earlier novel, so *Jane Eyre* is now haunted by Rhys's novel. *Wide Sargasso Sea* is a perfect example of inter-textuality and is also often cited as an example of a post-colonial novel. It appears in almost every book on critical theory, and it is a popular text in syllabuses at school and university level. However, while it is interesting and enjoyable to find the links between the two books, and to see what a reading of the twentieth-century novel adds to our understanding of the nineteenth-century one, *Wide Sargasso Sea* can be read independently.

It is much more than just a textbook. It is a moving story about growing up and about love and marriage. It is beautifully written, full of wonderfully evocative descriptions of the Caribbean, of its colours and scents; and it conveys tremendous emotion and pathos. Dreamlike images resonate throughout the book: dresses, hair, mirrors, flights of steps, roads through the forest that are there and yet are not. It is a place where dreams become nightmares; where history cannot be forgotten, and where no one can be free of the past. Where even a honeymoon place is called 'Massacre'.

Everything in the society of the novel is questioned: reason, justice, madness, freedom. The overall feeling is one of great sadness and anger, that such things can happen. As Angela Smith says in her 1997 introduction to the novel, 'The unspeakable story of human beings claiming, without pity, to own each other, in slavery, marriage or parenthood, is the revenant that haunts the novel' (*Wide Sargasso Sea*, Harmondsworth: Penguin, p. xxiii).

Chronology

Jean Rhys's Life

1890 Born Ella Gwendoline Rees Williams at Roseau, Dominica, one of the Windward Islands, to a white Creole mother of Scottish and Irish descent, and a Welsh doctor father.

1907 Comes to England, to the Perse School for Girls in Cambridge.

1909 Two terms at Sir Herbert Beerbohm Tree's School of Dramatic Art but is forced to leave drama school when her father dies. Works as chorus girl.

1910–12 First affair, with Launcelot Hugh Smith (twenty years her senior).

1917 Meets Jean Lenglet, a Dutch-French poet.

1919 Marries. Moves to Paris.

1920 Her son William dies aged three weeks. Lives in Vienna, Budapest, Belgium, Paris.

1922 Daughter Maryvonne is born. Discovers Lenglet is a bigamist.

1924 Lenglet imprisoned for currency offences. Rhys meets Ford Madox Ford, who encourages her writing. Becomes Ford's mistress. 'Vienne', her first published story, appears in *The Transatlantic Review*, edited by Ford, under the name Jean Rhys.

1927 *The Left Bank, and other stories* published in UK and USA. Leslie Tilden Smith becomes her literary agent.

1928 *Postures*, later published as *Quartet* (as in the USA). Starts living with Tilden Smith.

Jean Rhys's Times

1914–18 First World War.

1921 James Joyce publishes *Ulysses*.
1922 T. S. Eliot publishes *The Waste Land*.

1930 *Leaving Mr Mackenzie* (UK).

1931 *Leaving Mr Mackenzie* (USA).

1933 Divorces Lenglet.

1934 *Voyage in the Dark*. Marries Tilden Smith.

1936 Visits Dominica.

1939 *Good Morning, Midnight*.

1945 Tilden Smith dies. Maryvonne marries.

1946 Rhys and Max Hamer start living together in Beckenham.

1947 They marry.

1949 Rhys is rediscovered through an advert in the *New Statesman*.

1950–52 Hamer imprisoned for minor fraud.

1955 Move to Cornwall and living in poverty.

1957 Adaptation of *Good Morning, Midnight* broadcast by the BBC. Rhys signs contract with André Deutsch for *Wide Sargasso Sea*.

1960 Move to Devon. Publishes two stories in the *London Magazine*.

1966 Hamer dies. *WSS* published in UK and wins W. H. Smith prize. All her other books are now republished.

1967 *WSS* published in USA.

1968 *Tigers are Better-Looking* (stories).

1975 *My Day* published in the USA (three autobiographical pieces).

1976 *Sleep It Off Lady* (stories) published in UK and USA.

1979 Rhys dies. *Smile Please* (autobiography) published posthumously in UK and USA.

1931   Virginia Woolf publishes *The Waves*.

1936   Rosamund Lehmann publishes *The Weather in the Streets*.
1939–45   Second World War.

1947   George Orwell publishes *Nineteen Eighty-Four*.

1954   William Golding publishes *Lord of the Flies*.

1961   Muriel Spark publishes *The Prime of Miss Jean Brodie*.

Antoinette Cosway vs. Antoinette Mason
→ which one is preferred / right?

FAMILY HISTORY

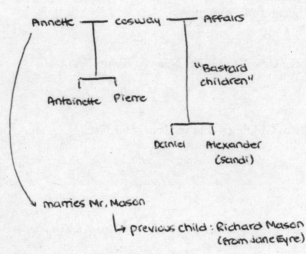

Annette ── Cosway ── Affairs

"Bastard children"

Antoinette   Pierre

Daniel   Alexander (Sandi)

→ marries Mr. Mason
    ↳ previous child: Richard Mason
        (from Jane Eyre)

hope for a new situation
    with Mason
Couldn = Gateshead
Convent = Lowood

Wide Sargasso Sea

• stratification - where people fit in.

- white people (new immigrants)
- creole : white people who have lived in Jamaica for a long time.
- Jamaican : indigenous, coloured
- christophene : 'blue black'

outsider, alienated, ostracized, foreigner, heirarchy

Part One ⊳ entirely chronological (youth → growing up)

rumor and innuendo   who is saying something and what are they saying

They say when trouble comes close ranks, and so the white people did. But we were not in their ranks. The Jamaican ladies had never approved of my mother, 'because she pretty like pretty self' Christophine said.   opens the novel

She was my father's second wife, far too young for him they thought, and, worse still, a Martinique girl. When I asked her why so few people came to see us, she told me that the road [TRAVEL] from Spanish Town to Coulibri Estate where we lived was very bad and that road repairing was now a thing of the past. (My father, visitors, horses, feeling safe in bed – all belonged to the past.) owns the plantation

Another day I heard her talking to Mr Luttrell, our neighbour and her only friend. 'Of course they have their own misfortunes. Still waiting for this compensation the English promised when the Emancipation Act was passed. Some will wait for a long time.'

How could she know that Mr Luttrell would be the first who grew tired of waiting? One calm evening he shot his dog, swam out to sea and was gone for always. No agent came from England to look after his property – Nelson's Rest it was called – and strangers from Spanish Town rode up to gossip and discuss the tragedy.

'Live at Nelson's Rest? Not for love or money. An unlucky place.'

Mr Luttrell's house was left empty, shutters banging in the wind. Soon the black people said it was haunted, they wouldn't go near it. And no one came near us.

I got used to a solitary life, but my mother still planned and hoped – perhaps she had to hope every time she passed a looking-glass. ⊳ sees an alter-ego in the mirror, one who lives with prosperity and opportunity.

3

Wide Sargasso Sea

She still rode about every morning not caring that the black people stood about in groups to jeer at her, especially after her riding clothes grew shabby (they notice clothes, they know about money). *becomes the evil of the world*

5 Then one day, very early, I saw her horse lying down under the frangipani tree. I went up to him but he was not sick, he was dead and his eyes were black with flies. I ran away and did not speak of it for I thought if I told no one it might not be true. But later that day, Godfrey found him, he had been poisoned. 'Now we are

10 marooned,' my mother said, 'now what will become of us?'

Godfrey said, 'I can't watch the horse night and day. I too old now. When the old time go, let it go. No use to grab at it. The Lord make no distinction between black and white, black and white the same for Him. Rest yourself in peace for the righteous

15 are not forsaken.' But she couldn't. She was young. How could she not try for all the things that had gone so suddenly, so without warning. 'You're blind when you want to be blind,' she said ferociously, 'and you're deaf when you want to be deaf. The old hypocrite,' she kept saying. 'He knew what they were going to do.'

20 'The devil prince of this world,' Godfrey said, 'but this world don't last so long for mortal man.'

She persuaded a Spanish Town doctor to visit my younger brother Pierre who staggered when he walked and couldn't speak distinctly. I don't know what the doctor told her or what she

25 said to him but he never came again and after that she changed. Suddenly, not gradually. She grew thin and silent, and at last she refused to leave the house at all.

Our garden was large and beautiful as that garden in the Bible – the tree of life grew there. But it had gone wild. The paths were

30 overgrown and a smell of dead flowers mixed with the fresh living smell. Underneath the tree ferns, tall as forest tree ferns, the light was green. Orchids flourished out of reach or for some reason not to be touched. One was snaky looking, another like an octopus with long thin brown tentacles bare of leaves hanging from a twisted

35 root. Twice a year the octopus orchid flowered – then not an inch

allusion to the
4 garden of Eden

L phallic + feminine
references, foreshadows the passion
which Antoinette begins to feel for Rochester,
whereas before she strayed from temptation.

of tentacle showed. It was a bell-shaped mass of white, mauve, deep purples, wonderful to see. The scent was very sweet and strong. I never went near it.   ⌐ foreshadowing Antoinette 'going wild'

All Coulibri Estate had <u>gone wild</u> like the garden, gone to bush. No more slavery – why should *anybody* work? This never saddened   5
me. I did not remember the place when it was prosperous.

My mother usually walked up and down the *glacis*, a paved roofed-in terrace which ran the length of the house and sloped upwards to a clump of bamboos. Standing by the bamboos she had a clear view to the sea, but anyone passing could stare at her.   10
They stared, sometimes they laughed. Long after the sound was far away and faint she kept her eyes shut and her hands clenched. A frown came between her black eyebrows, deep – it might have been cut with a knife. I hated this frown and once I touched her forehead trying to smooth it. But she pushed me away, not roughly   15
but calmly, coldly, without a word, as if she had decided once and for all that I was useless to her. She wanted to sit with Pierre or walk where she pleased without being pestered, she wanted peace and quiet. I was old enough to look after myself. 'Oh, let me alone,' she would say, 'let me alone,' and after I knew that she talked aloud   20
to herself I was a little afraid of her.

So I spent most of my time in the kitchen which was in an outbuilding some way off. Christophine slept in the little room next to it.

When evening came she sang to me if she was in the mood. I   25
couldn't always understand her patois songs – she also came from Martinique – but she taught me the one that meant 'The little ones grow old, the children leave us, will they come back?' and the one about the cedar tree flowers which only last for a day.

The music was gay but the words were sad and her voice often   30
quavered and broke on the high note. 'Adieu.' Not adieu as we said it, but *à dieu*, which made more sense after all. The loving man was lonely, the girl was deserted, the children never came back. Adieu.

Her songs were not like Jamaican songs, and she was not like the   35
other women.

Christophene's use of language is significant.

She was much blacker – blue-black with a thin face and straight features. She wore a black dress, heavy gold earrings and a yellow handkerchief – carefully tied with the two high points in front. No other negro woman wore black, or tied her handkerchief Mar-
5 tinique fashion. She had a quiet voice and a quiet laugh (when she did laugh), and though she could speak good English if she wanted to, and French as well as patois, she took care to talk as they talked. But they would have nothing to do with her and she never saw her son who worked in Spanish Town. She had only one friend – a
10 woman called Maillotte, and Maillotte was not a Jamaican.

The girls from the bayside who sometimes helped with the washing and cleaning were terrified of her. That, I soon discovered, was why they came at all – for she never paid them. Yet they brought presents of fruit and vegetables and after dark I often heard
15 low voices from the kitchen.

So I asked about Christophine. Was she very old? Had she always been with us?

'She was your father's wedding present to me – one of his presents. He thought I would be pleased with a Martinique girl. I
20 don't know how old she was when they brought her to Jamaica, quite young. I don't know how old she is now. Does it matter? Why do you pester and bother me about all these things that happened long ago? Christophine stayed with me because she wanted to stay. She had her own very good reasons you may be
25 sure. I dare say we would have died if she'd turned against us and that would have been a better fate. To die and be forgotten and at peace. Not to know that one is abandoned, lied about, helpless. All the ones who died – who says a good word for them now?'

'Godfrey stayed too,' I said. 'And Sass.'

30 'They stayed,' she said angrily, 'because they wanted somewhere to sleep and something to eat. That boy Sass! When his mother pranced off and left him here – a great deal *she* cared – why he was a little skeleton. Now he's growing into a big strong boy and away he goes. We shan't see him again. Godfrey is a rascal. These new
35 ones aren't too kind to old people and he knows it. That's why he stays. Doesn't do a thing but eats enough for a couple of horses.

6

opening section // to Gateshead

are @ coulibri ⌐ *red room*

Pretends he's deaf. He isn't deaf – he doesn't want to hear. What a devil he is!'

'Why don't you tell him to find somewhere else to live?' I said and she laughed.

'He wouldn't go. He'd probably try to force us out. I've learned 5
to let sleeping curs lie,' she said.

'Would Christophine go if you told her to?' I thought. But I didn't say it. I was afraid to say it.

It was too hot that afternoon. I could see the beads of perspiration on her upper lip and the dark circles under her eyes. I started to 10
fan her, but she turned her head away. She might rest if I left her alone, she said.

Once I would have gone back quietly to watch her asleep on the blue sofa – once I made excuses to be near her when she brushed her hair, a soft black cloak to cover me, hide me, keep me safe. 15

But not any longer. Not any more.

These were all the people in my life – my mother and Pierre, Christophine, Godfrey, and Sass who had left us.

I never looked at any strange negro. They hated us. They called us white cockroaches. Let sleeping curs lie. One day a little girl followed 20
me singing, 'Go away white cockroach, go away, go away.' I walked fast, but she walked faster. 'White cockroach, go away, go away. Nobody want you. Go away.'

When I was safely home I sat close to the old wall at the end of the garden. It was covered with green moss soft as velvet and I 25
never wanted to move again. Everything would be worse if I moved. Christophine found me there when it was nearly dark, and I was so stiff she had to help me to get up. She said nothing, but next morning Tia was in the kitchen with her mother Maillotte, Christophine's friend. Soon Tia was my friend and I met her nearly 30
every morning at the turn of the road to the river.

Sometimes we left the bathing pool at midday, sometimes we stayed till late afternoon. Then Tia would light a fire (fires always lit for her, sharp stones did not hurt her bare feet, I never saw her cry). We boiled green bananas in an old iron pot and ate them with 35

our fingers out of a calabash and after we had eaten she slept at once. I could not sleep, but I wasn't quite awake as I lay in the shade looking at the pool – deep and dark green under the trees, brown-green if it had rained, but a bright sparkling green in the
5 sun. The water was so clear that you could see the pebbles at the bottom of the shallow part. Blue and white and striped red. Very pretty. Late or early we parted at the turn of the road. My mother never asked me where I had been or what I had done.
   Christophine had given me some new pennies which I kept in
10 the pocket of my dress. They dropped out one morning so I put them on a stone. They shone like gold in the sun and Tia stared. She had small eyes, very black, set deep in her head.
   Then she bet me three of the pennies that I couldn't turn a somersault under water 'like you say you can'.
15 'Of course I can.'
   'I never see you do it,' she said. 'Only talk.'
   'Bet you all the money I can,' I said.
   But after one somersault I still turned and came up choking. Tia laughed and told me that it certainly look like I drown dead that
20 time. Then she picked up the money.
   'I did do it,' I said when I could speak but she shook her head. I hadn't done it good and besides pennies didn't buy much. Why did I look at her like that?
   'Keep them then, you cheating nigger,' I said, for I was tired,
25 and the water I had swallowed made me feel sick. 'I can get more if I want to.'
   That's not what she hear, she said. She hear all we poor like beggar. We ate salt fish – no money for fresh fish. That old house so leaky, you run with calabash to catch water when it rain. Plenty
30 white people in Jamaica. Real white people, they got gold money. They didn't look at us, nobody see them come near us. Old time white people nothing but white nigger now, and black nigger better than white nigger.
   I wrapped myself in my torn towel and sat on a stone with my
35 back to her, shivering cold. But the sun couldn't warm me. I wanted to go home. I looked round and Tia had gone. I searched

for a long time before I could believe that she had taken my dress – not my underclothes, she never wore any – but my dress, starched, ironed, clean that morning. She had left me hers and I put it on at last and walked home in the blazing sun feeling sick, hating her. I planned to get round the back of the house to the kitchen, but 5 passing the stables I stopped to stare at three strange horses and my mother saw me and called. She was on the *glacis* with two young ladies and a gentleman. Visitors! I dragged up the steps unwillingly – I had longed for visitors once, but that was years ago. 10

They were very beautiful I thought and they wore such beautiful clothes that I looked away down at the flagstones and when they laughed – the gentleman laughed the loudest – I ran into the house, into my bedroom. There I stood with my back against the door and I could feel my heart all through me. I heard them talking and 15 I heard them leave. I came out of my room and my mother was sitting on the blue sofa. She looked at me for some time before she said that I had behaved very oddly. My dress was even dirtier than usual.

'It's Tia's dress.' 20

'But why are you wearing Tia's dress? Tia? Which one of them is Tia?'

Christophine, who had been in the pantry listening, came at once and was told to find a clean dress for me. 'Throw away that thing. Burn it.' 25

Then they quarrelled.

Christophine said I had no clean dress. 'She got two dresses, wash and wear. You want clean dress to drop from heaven? Some people crazy in truth.'

'She must have another dress,' said my mother. 'Somewhere.' 30 But Christophine told her loudly that it shameful. She run wild, she grow up worthless. And nobody care.

My mother walked over to the window. ('Marooned,' said her straight narrow back, her carefully coiled hair. 'Marooned.')

'She has an old muslin dress. Find that.' 35

While Christophine scrubbed my face and tied my plaits with a fresh piece of string, she told me that those were the new people at Nelson's Rest. They called themselves Luttrell, but English or not English they were not like old Mr Luttrell. 'Old Mr Luttrell spit in their face if he see how they look at you. Trouble walk into the house this day. Trouble walk in.'

The old muslin dress was found and it tore as I forced it on. She didn't notice.

No more slavery! She had to laugh! 'These new ones have Letter of the Law. Same thing. They got magistrate. They got fine. They got jail house and chain gang. They got tread machine to mash up people's feet. New ones worse than old ones – more cunning, that's all.'

All that evening my mother didn't speak to me or look at me and I thought, 'She is ashamed of me, what Tia said is true.'

I went to bed early and slept at once. I dreamed that I was walking in the forest. Not alone. Someone who hated me was with me, out of sight. I could hear heavy footsteps coming closer and though I struggled and screamed I could not move. I woke crying. The covering sheet was on the floor and my mother was looking down at me.

'Did you have a nightmare?'

'Yes, a bad dream.'

> concern for Pierre because he is the male heir, the power of her estate (future livelyhood)

She sighed and covered me up. 'You were making such a noise. I must go to Pierre, you've frightened him.'

I lay thinking, 'I am safe. There is the corner of the bedroom door and the friendly furniture. There is the tree of life in the garden and the wall green with moss. The barrier of the cliffs and the high mountains. And the barrier of the sea. I am safe. I am safe from strangers.'

The light of the candle in Pierre's room was still there when I slept again. I woke next morning knowing that nothing would be the same. It would change and go on changing.

I don't know how she got money to buy the white muslin and the pink. Yards of muslin. She may have sold her last ring, for there was one left. I saw it in her jewel box – that, and a locket with a shamrock inside. They were mending and sewing first thing in the

morning and still sewing when I went to bed. In a week she had a
new dress and so had I.

The Luttrells lent her a horse, and she would ride off very early
and not come back till late next day – tired out because she had
been to a dance or a moonlight picnic. She was gay and laughing   5
– younger than I had ever seen her and the house was sad when
she had gone.

So I too left it and stayed away till dark. I was never long at the
bathing pool, I never met Tia.

I took another road, past the old sugar works and the water   10
wheel that had not turned for years. I went to parts of Coulibri that
I had not seen, where there was no road, no path, no track. And if
the razor grass cut my legs and arms I would think 'It's better than
people.' Black ants or red ones, tall nests swarming with white
ants, rain that soaked me to the skin – once I saw a snake. All better 15
than people.

Better. Better, better than people.

Watching the red and yellow flowers in the sun thinking of
nothing, it was as if a door opened and I was somewhere else,
something else. Not myself any longer.   20

I knew the time of day when though it is hot and blue and there
are no clouds, the sky can have a very black look.

I was bridesmaid when my mother married Mr Mason in Spanish
Town. Christophine curled my hair. I carried a bouquet and everything I wore was new – even my beautiful slippers. But their eyes 25
slid away from my hating face. I had heard what all these smooth
smiling people said about her when she was not listening and they
did not guess I was. Hiding from them in the garden when they
visited Coulibri, I listened.

'A fantastic marriage and he will regret it. Why should a very   30
wealthy man who could take his pick of all the girls in the West
Indies, and many in England too probably?' 'Why *probably*?' the
other voice said. '*Certainly*.' 'Then why should he marry a widow
without a penny to her name and Coulibri a wreck of a place?
Emancipation troubles killed old Cosway? Nonsense – the estate   35

was going downhill for years before that. He drank himself to
death. Many's the time when – well! And all those women! She
never did anything to stop him – she encouraged him. Presents
and smiles for the bastards every Christmas. Old customs? Some
5 old customs are better dead and buried. Her new husband will
have to spend a pretty penny before the house is fit to live in – leaks
like a sieve. And what about the stables and the coach house dark
as pitch, and the servants' quarters and the six-foot snake I saw
with my own eyes curled up on the privy seat last time I was here.
10 Alarmed? I screamed. Then that horrible old man she harbours
came along, doubled up with laughter. As for those two children –
the boy an idiot kept out of sight and mind and the girl going the
same way in my opinion – a *lowering* expression.'

'Oh I agree,' the other one said, 'but Annette is such a pretty
15 woman. And what a dancer. Reminds me of that song "light as
cotton blossom on the something breeze", or is it air? I forget.'

Yes, what a dancer – that night when they came home from their
honeymoon in Trinidad and they danced on the *glacis* to no music.
There was no need for music when she danced. They stopped and
20 she leaned backwards over his arm, down till her black hair touched
the flagstones – still down, down. Then up again in a flash, laughing. She made it look so easy – as if anyone could do it, and he
kissed her – a long kiss. I was there that time too but they had
forgotten me and soon I wasn't thinking of them. I was remem-
25 bering that woman saying 'Dance! He didn't come to the West
Indies to dance – he came to make money as they all do. Some of
the big estates are going cheap, and one unfortunate's loss is always
a clever man's gain. No, the whole thing is a mystery. It's evidently
useful to keep a Martinique obeah woman on the premises.' She
30 meant Christophine. She said it mockingly, not meaning it, but
soon other people were saying it – and meaning it.

While the repairs were being done and they were in Trinidad,
Pierre and I stayed with Aunt Cora in Spanish Town.

Mr Mason did not approve of Aunt Cora, an ex-slave-owner
35 who had escaped misery, a flier in the face of Providence.

'Why did she do nothing to help you?'

I told him that her husband was English and didn't like us and he said, 'Nonsense.'

'It isn't nonsense, they lived in England and he was angry if she wrote to us. He hated the West Indies. When he died not long ago   5
she came home, before that what could she do? *She* wasn't rich.'

'That's her story. I don't believe it. A frivolous woman. In your mother's place I'd resent her behaviour.'

'None of you understand about us,' I thought.

Coulibri looked the same when I saw it again, although it was   10
clean and tidy, no grass between the flagstones, no leaks. But it didn't feel the same. Sass had come back and I was glad. They can *smell* money, somebody said. Mr Mason engaged new servants – I didn't like any of them excepting Mannie the groom. It was their talk about Christophine that changed Coulibri, not the repairs   15
or the new furniture or the strange faces. Their talk about Christophine and obeah changed it.

I knew her room so well – the pictures of the Holy Family and the prayer for a happy death. She had a bright patchwork counterpane, a broken-down press for her clothes, and my mother   20
had given her an old rocking-chair.

Yet one day when I was waiting there I was suddenly very much afraid. The door was open to the sunlight, someone was whistling near the stables, but I was afraid. I was certain that hidden in the room (behind the old black press?) there was a dead man's dried   25
hand, white chicken feathers, a cock with its throat cut, dying slowly, slowly. Drop by drop the blood was falling into a red basin and I imagined I could hear it. No one had ever spoken to me about obeah – but I knew what I would find if I dared to look. Then Christophine came in smiling and pleased to see me. Nothing   30
alarming ever happened and I forgot, or told myself I had forgotten.

Mr Mason would laugh if he knew how frightened I had been. He would laugh even louder than he did when my mother told him that she wished to leave Coulibri.

This began when they had been married for over a year. They   35

always said the same things and I seldom listened to the argument
now. I knew that we were hated – but to go away ... for once I
agreed with my stepfather. That was not possible.

'You must have some reason,' he would say, and she would
5 answer 'I need a change' or 'We could visit Richard.' (Richard, Mr
Mason's son by his first marriage, was at school in Barbados. He
was going to England soon and we had seen very little of him.)

'An agent could look after this place. For the time being. The
people here hate us. They certainly hate me.' Straight out she said
10 that one day and it was then he laughed so heartily.

'Annette, be reasonable. You were the widow of a slave-owner,
the daughter of a slave-owner, and you had been living here alone,
with two children, for nearly five years when we met. Things were
at their worst then. But you were never molested, never harmed.'

15 'How do you know that I was not harmed?' she said. 'We were
so poor then,' she told him, 'we were something to laugh at. But
we are not poor now,' she said. 'You are not a poor man. Do you
suppose that they don't know all about your estate in Trinidad?
And the Antigua property? They talk about us without stopping.
20 They invent stories about you, and lies about me. They try to find
out what we eat every day.'

'They are curious. It's natural enough. You have lived alone far
too long, Annette. You imagine enmity which doesn't exist. Always
one extreme or the other. Didn't you fly at me like a little wild cat
25 when I said nigger. Not nigger, nor even Negro. Black people I
must say.'

'You don't like, or even recognize, the good in them,' she said,
'and you won't believe in the other side.'

'They're too damn lazy to be dangerous,' said Mr Mason. 'I
30 know that.'

'They are more alive than you are, lazy or not, and they can be
dangerous and cruel for reasons you wouldn't understand.'

'No, I don't understand,' Mr Mason always said. 'I don't understand at all.'

35 But she'd speak about going away again. Persistently. Angrily.

★

Mr Mason pulled up near the empty huts on our way home that evening. 'All gone to one of those dances,' he said. 'Young and old. How deserted the place looks.'

'We'll hear the drums if there is a dance.' I hoped he'd ride on quickly but he stayed by the huts to watch the sun go down, the sky and the sea were on fire when we left Bertrand Bay at last. From a long way off I saw the shadow of our house high up on its stone foundations. There was a smell of ferns and river water and I felt safe again, as if I was one of the righteous. (Godfrey said that we were not righteous. One day when he was drunk he told me that we were all damned and no use praying.)

'They've chosen a very hot night for their dance,' Mr Mason said, and Aunt Cora came on to the *glacis*. 'What dance? Where?'

'There is some festivity in the neighbourhood. The huts were abandoned. A wedding perhaps?'

'Not a wedding,' I said. 'There is never a wedding.' He frowned at me but Aunt Cora smiled.

When they had gone indoors I leaned my arms on the cool *glacis* railings and thought that I would never like him very much. I still called him 'Mr Mason' in my head. 'Goodnight white pappy,' I said one evening and he was not vexed, he laughed. In some ways it was better before he came though he'd rescued us from poverty and misery. 'Only just in time too.' The black people did not hate us quite so much when we were poor. We were white but we had not escaped and soon we would be dead for we had no money left. What was there to hate?

Now it had started up again and worse than before, my mother knows but she can't make him believe it. I wish I could tell him that out here is not at all like English people think it is. I wish . . .

I could hear them talking and Aunt Cora's laugh. I was glad she was staying with us. And I could hear the bamboos shiver and creak though there was no wind. It had been hot and still and dry for days. The colours had gone from the sky, the light was blue and could not last long. The *glacis* was not a good place when night was coming, Christophine said. As I went indoors my mother was talking in an excited voice.

'Very well. As you refuse to consider it, *I* will go and take Pierre with me. You won't object to that, I hope?'

'You are perfectly right, Annette,' said Aunt Cora and that did surprise me. She seldom spoke when they argued.

5 Mr Mason also seemed surprised and not at all pleased.

'You talk so wildly,' he said. 'And you are so mistaken. Of course you can get away for a change if you wish it. I promise you.'

'You have promised that before,' she said. 'You don't keep your promises.'

10 He sighed. 'I feel very well here. However, we'll arrange something. Quite soon.'

'I will not stay at Coulibri any longer,' my mother said. 'It is not safe. It is not safe for Pierre.'

Aunt Cora nodded.

15 As it was late I ate with them instead of by myself as usual. Myra, one of the new servants, was standing by the sideboard, waiting to change the plates. We ate English food now, beef and mutton, pies and puddings.

I was glad to be like an English girl but I missed the taste of
20 Christophine's cooking.

tension
between
the
working
classes

My stepfather talked about a plan to import labourers – coolies he called them – from the East Indies. When Myra had gone out Aunt Cora said, 'I shouldn't discuss that if I were you. Myra is listening.'

25 'But the people here won't work. They don't want to work. Look at this place – it's enough to break your heart.'

'Hearts have been broken,' she said. 'Be sure of that. I suppose you all know what you are doing.'

'Do you mean to say –'

30 'I said nothing, except that it would be wiser not to tell that woman your plans – necessary and merciful no doubt. I don't trust her.'

'Live here most of your life and know nothing about the people. It's astonishing. They are children – they wouldn't hurt a fly.'

35 'Unhappily children do hurt flies,' said Aunt Cora.

Myra came in again looking mournful as she always did though she smiled when she talked about hell. Everyone went to hell, she told me, you had to belong to her sect to be saved and even then – just as well not to be too sure. She had thin arms and big hands and feet and the handkerchief she wore round her head was always white. Never striped or a gay colour.   *// to the book Jane reads in G-head*

So I looked away from her at my favourite picture, 'The Miller's Daughter', a lovely English girl with brown curls and blue eyes and a dress slipping off her shoulders. Then I looked across the white tablecloth and the vase of yellow roses at Mr Mason, so sure of himself, so without a doubt English. And at my mother, so without a doubt not English, but no white nigger either. Not my mother. Never had been. Never could be. Yes, she would have died, I thought, if she had not met him. And for the first time I was grateful and liked him. There are more ways than one of being happy, better perhaps to be peaceful and contented and protected, as I feel now, peaceful for years and long years, and afterwards I may be saved whatever Myra says. (When I asked Christophine what happened when you died, she said, 'You want to know too much.') I remembered to kiss my stepfather goodnight. Once Aunt Cora had told me, 'He's very hurt because you never kiss him.'

'He does not look hurt,' I argued. 'Great mistake to go by looks,' she said, 'one way or the other.'

I went into Pierre's room which was next to mine, the last one in the house. The bamboos were outside his window. You could almost touch them. He still had a crib and he slept more and more, nearly all the time. He was so thin that I could lift him easily. Mr Mason had promised to take him to England later on, there he would be cured, made like other people. 'And how will you like that?' I thought, as I kissed him. 'How will you like being made exactly like other people?' He looked happy asleep. But that will be later on. Later on. Sleep now. It was then I heard the bamboos creak again and a sound like whispering. I forced myself to look out of the window. There was a full moon but I saw nobody, nothing but shadows.

I left a light on the chair by my bed and waited for Christophine, for I liked to see her last thing. But she did not come, and as the

→ comfort and hope for Antoinette, very English picture.

candle burned down, the safe peaceful feeling left me. I wished I had a big Cuban dog to lie by my bed and protect me, I wished I had not heard a noise by the bamboo clump, or that I were very young again, for then I believed in my stick. It was not a stick, but
5 a long narrow piece of wood, with two nails sticking out at the end, a shingle, perhaps. I picked it up soon after they killed our horse and I thought I can fight with this, if the worst comes to the worst I can fight to the end though the best ones fall and that is another song. Christophine knocked the nails out, but she let me keep the
10 shingle and I grew very fond of it, I believed that no one could harm me when it was near me, to lose it would be a great misfortune. All this was long ago, when I was still babyish and sure that everything was alive, not only the river or the rain, but chairs, looking-glasses, cups, saucers, everything.
15 I woke up and it was still night and my mother was there. She said, 'Get up and dress yourself, and come downstairs quickly.' She was dressed, but she had not put up her hair and one of her plaits was loose. 'Quickly,' she said again, then she went into Pierre's room, next door. I heard her speak to Myra and I heard
20 Myra answer her. I lay there, half asleep, looking at the lighted candle on the chest of drawers, till I heard a noise as though a chair had fallen over in the little room, then I got up and dressed.

The house was on different levels. There were three steps down from my bedroom and Pierre's to the dining-room and then three
25 steps from the dining-room to the rest of the house, which we called 'downstairs'. The folding doors of the dining-room were not shut and I could see that the big drawing-room was full of people. Mr Mason, my mother, Christophine and Mannie and Sass. Aunt Cora was sitting on the blue sofa in the corner now, wearing a
30 black silk dress, her ringlets were carefully arranged. She looked very haughty, I thought. But Godfrey was not there, or Myra, or the cook, or any of the others.

'There is no reason to be alarmed,' my stepfather was saying as I came in. 'A handful of drunken negroes.' He opened the door
35 leading to the *glacis* and walked out. 'What is all this,' he shouted.

'What do you want?' A horrible noise swelled up, like animals howling, but worse. We heard stones falling on to the *glacis*. He was pale when he came in again, but he tried to smile as he shut and bolted the door. 'More of them than I thought, and in a nasty mood too. They will repent in the morning. I foresee gifts of tamarinds in syrup and ginger sweets tomorrow.'

'Tomorrow will be too late,' said Aunt Cora, 'too late for ginger sweets or anything else.' My mother was not listening to either of them. She said, 'Pierre is asleep and Myra is with him, I thought it better to leave him in his own room, away from this horrible noise. I don't know. Perhaps.' She was twisting her hands together, her wedding ring fell off and rolled into a corner near the steps. My stepfather and Mannie both stooped for it, then Mannie straightened up and said, 'Oh, my God, they get at the back, they set fire to the back of the house.' He pointed to my bedroom door which I had shut after me, and smoke was rolling out from underneath.

I did not see my mother move she was so quick. She opened the door of my room and then again I did not see her, nothing but smoke. Mannie ran after her, so did Mr Mason but more slowly. Aunt Cora put her arms round me. She said, 'Don't be afraid, you are quite safe. We are all quite safe.' Just for a moment I shut my eyes and rested my head against her shoulder. She smelled of vanilla, I remember. Then there was another smell, of burned hair, and I looked and my mother was in the room carrying Pierre. It was her loose hair that had burned and was smelling like that.

I thought, Pierre is dead. He looked dead. He was white and he did not make a sound, but his head hung back over her arm as if he had no life at all and his eyes were rolled up so that you only saw the whites. My stepfather said, 'Annette, you are hurt – your hands . . .' But she did not even look at him. 'His crib was on fire,' she said to Aunt Cora. 'The little room is on fire and Myra was not there. She has gone. She was not there.'

'That does not surprise me at all,' said Aunt Cora. She laid Pierre on the sofa, bent over him, then lifted up her skirt, stepped out of her white petticoat and began to tear it into strips.

'She left him, she ran away and left him alone to die,' said my

mother, still whispering. So it was all the more dreadful when she
began to scream abuse at Mr Mason, calling him a fool, a cruel
stupid fool. 'I told you,' she said, 'I told you what would happen
again and again.' Her voice broke, but still she screamed, 'You
5 would not listen, you sneered at me, you grinning hypocrite, you
ought not to live either, you know so much, don't you? Why don't
you go out and ask them to let you go? Say how innocent you are.
Say you have always trusted them.'

I was so shocked that everything was confused. And it happened
10 quickly. I saw Mannie and Sass staggering along with two large
earthenware jars of water which were kept in the pantry. They
threw the water into the bedroom and it made a black pool on the
floor, but the smoke rolled over the pool. Then Christophine, who
had run into my mother's bedroom for the pitcher there, came
15 back and spoke to my aunt. 'It seems they have fired the other side
of the house,' said Aunt Cora. 'They must have climbed that tree
outside. This place is going to burn like tinder and there is nothing
we can do to stop it. The sooner we get out the better.'

Mannie said to the boy, 'You frightened?' Sass shook his head.
20 'Then come on,' said Mannie. 'Out of my way,' he said and pushed
Mr Mason aside. Narrow wooden stairs led down from the pantry
to the outbuildings, the kitchen, the servants' rooms, the stables.
That was where they were going. 'Take the child,' Aunt Cora told
Christophine, 'and come.'

25 It was very hot on the *glacis* too, they roared as we came out,
then there was another roar behind us. I had not seen any flames,
only smoke and sparks, but now I saw tall flames shooting up to
the sky, for the bamboos had caught. There were some tree ferns
near, green and damp, one of those was smouldering too.

30 'Come quickly,' said Aunt Cora, and she went first, holding my
hand. Christophine followed, carrying Pierre, and they were quite
silent as we went down the *glacis* steps. But when I looked round
for my mother I saw that Mr Mason, his face crimson with heat,
seemed to be dragging her along and she was holding back,
35 struggling. I heard him say, 'It's impossible, too late now.'

'Wants her jewel case?' Aunt Cora said.

'Jewel case? Nothing so sensible,' bawled Mr Mason. 'She wanted to go back for her damned parrot. I won't allow it.' She did not answer, only fought him silently, twisting like a cat and showing her teeth. *knows who he is ∴ has his own identity / Ché coco? c'est coco = its coco*

Our parrot was called Coco, a green parrot. He didn't talk very 5 well, he could say *Qui est là? Qui est là?* and answer himself *Ché Coco, Ché Coco.* After Mr Mason clipped his wings he grew very bad tempered, and though he would sit quietly on my mother's shoulder, he darted at everyone who came near her and pecked their feet. 10

'Annette,' said Aunt Cora. 'They are laughing at you, do not allow them to laugh at you.' She stopped fighting then and he half supported, half pulled her after us, cursing loudly.

Still they were quiet and there were so many of them I could hardly see any grass or trees. There must have been many of the 15 bay people but I recognized no one. They all looked the same, it was the same face repeated over and over, eyes gleaming, mouth half open to shout. We were past the mounting stone when they saw Mannie driving the carriage round the corner. Sass followed, riding one horse and leading another. There was a ladies' saddle 20 on the one he was leading.

Somebody yelled, 'But look the black Englishman! Look the white niggers!', and then they were all yelling. 'Look the white niggers! Look the damn white niggers!' A stone just missed Mannie's head, he cursed back at them and they cleared away from the rearing, 25 frightened horses. 'Come on, for God's sake,' said Mr Mason. 'Get to the carriage, get to the horses.' But we could not move for they pressed too close round us. Some of them were laughing and waving sticks, some of the ones at the back were carrying flambeaux and it was light as day. Aunt Cora held my hand very tightly and 30 her lips moved but I could not hear because of the noise. And I was afraid, because I knew that the ones who laughed would be the worst. I shut my eyes and waited. Mr Mason stopped swearing and began to pray in a loud pious voice. The prayer ended, 'May Almighty God defend us.' And God who is indeed mysterious, 35 who had made no sign when they burned Pierre as he slept – not a clap of thunder, not a flash of lightning – mysterious God heard Mr Mason at once and answered him. The yells stopped.

I opened my eyes, everybody was looking up and pointing at Coco on the *glacis* railings with his feathers alight. He made an effort to fly down but his clipped wings failed him and he fell screeching. He was all on fire.

I began to cry. 'Don't look,' said Aunt Cora. 'Don't look.' She stooped and put her arms round me and I hid my face, but I could feel that they were not so near. I heard someone say something about bad luck and remembered that it was very unlucky to kill a parrot, or even to see a parrot die. They began to go then, quickly, silently, and those that were left drew aside and watched us as we trailed across the grass. They were not laughing any more.

'Get to the carriage, get to the carriage,' said Mr Mason. 'Hurry!' He went first, holding my mother's arm, then Christophine carrying Pierre, and Aunt Cora was last, still with my hand in hers. None of us looked back.

Mannie had stopped the horses at the bend of the cobblestone road and as we got closer we heard him shout, 'What all you are, eh? Brute beasts?' He was speaking to a group of men and a few women who were standing round the carriage. A coloured man with a machete in his hand was holding the bridle. I did not see Sass or the other two horses. 'Get in,' said Mr Mason. 'Take no notice of him, get in.' The man with the machete said no. We would go to police and tell a lot of damn lies. A woman said to let us go. All this an accident and they had plenty witness. 'Myra she witness for us.'

'Shut your mouth,' the man said. 'You mash centipede, mash it, leave one little piece and it grow again . . . What you think police believe, eh? You, or the white nigger?'

Mr Mason stared at him. He seemed not frightened, but too astounded to speak. Mannie took up the carriage whip but one of the blacker men wrenched it out of his hand, snapped it over his knee and threw it away. 'Run away, black Englishman, like the boy run. Hide in the bushes. It's better for you.' It was Aunt Cora who stepped forward and said, 'The little boy is very badly hurt. He will die if we cannot get help for him.'

The man said, 'So black and white, they burn the same, eh?'

'They do,' she said. 'Here and hereafter, as you will find out. Very shortly.'

He let the bridle go and thrust his face close to hers. He'd throw her on the fire, he said, if she put bad luck on him. Old white jumby, he called her. But she did not move an inch, she looked straight into his eyes and threatened him with eternal fire in a calm voice. 'And never a drop of sangoree to cool your burning tongue,' she said. He cursed her again but he backed away. 'Now get in,' said Mr Mason. 'You, Christophine, get in with the child.' Christophine got in. 'Now you,' he said to my mother. But she had turned and was looking back at the house and when he put his hand on her arm, she screamed.

One woman said she only come to see what happen. Another woman began to cry. The man with the cutlass said, 'You cry for her – when she ever cry for you? Tell me that.'

But now I turned too. The house was burning, the yellow-red sky was like sunset and I knew that I would never see Coulibri again. Nothing would be left, the golden ferns and the silver ferns, the orchids, the ginger lilies and the roses, the rocking-chairs and the blue sofa, the jasmine and the honeysuckle, and the picture of the Miller's Daughter. When they had finished, there would be nothing left but blackened walls and the mounting stone. That was always left. That could not be stolen or burned.

Then, not so far off, I saw Tia and her mother and I ran to her, for she was all that was left of my life as it had been. We had eaten the same food, slept side by side, bathed in the same river. As I ran, I thought, I will live with Tia and I will be like her. Not to leave Coulibri. Not to go. Not. When I was close I saw the jagged stone in her hand but I did not see her throw it. I did not feel it either, only something wet, running down my face. I looked at her and I saw her face crumple up as she began to cry. We stared at each other, blood on my face, tears on hers. It was as if I saw myself. Like in a looking-glass.

*

'I saw my plait, tied with red ribbon, when I got up,' I said. 'In the chest of drawers. I thought it was a snake.'

'Your hair had to be cut. You've been very ill, my darling,' said Aunt Cora. 'But you are safe with me now. We are all safe as I told
5 you we would be. You must stay in bed though. Why are you wandering about the room? Your hair will grow again,' she said. 'Longer and thicker.'

'But darker,' I said.

'Why not darker?'

10 She picked me up and I was glad to feel the soft mattress and glad to be covered with a cool sheet.

'It's time for your arrowroot,' she said and went out. When that was finished she took the cup away and stood looking down at me.

15 'I got up because I wanted to know where I was.'

'And you do know, don't you?' she said in an anxious voice.

'Of course. But how did I get to your house?'

'The Luttrells were very good. As soon as Mannie got to Nelson's Rest they sent a hammock and four men. You were shaken about
20 a good deal though. But they did their best. Young Mr Luttrell rode alongside you all the way. Wasn't that kind?'

'Yes,' I said. She looked thin and old and her hair wasn't arranged prettily so I shut my eyes, not wanting to see her.

'Pierre is dead, isn't he?'

25 'He died on the way down, the poor little boy,' she said.

'He died before that,' I thought but was too tired to speak.

'Your mother is in the country. Resting. Getting well again. You will see her quite soon.'

'I didn't know,' I said. 'Why did she go away?'

30 'You've been very ill for nearly six weeks. You didn't know anything.'

What was the use of telling her that I'd been awake before and heard my mother screaming '*Qui est là? Qui est là?*' then 'Don't touch me. I'll kill you if you touch me. Coward. Hypocrite. I'll kill
35 you.' I'd put my hands over my ears, her screams were so loud and terrible. I slept and when I woke up everything was quiet.

Still Aunt Cora stayed by my bed looking at me.

'My head is bandaged up. It's so hot,' I said. 'Will I have a mark on my forehead?'

'No, no.' She smiled for the first time. 'That is healing very nicely. It won't spoil you on your wedding day,' she said.

She bent down and kissed me. 'Is there anything you want? A cool drink to sip?'

'No, not a drink. Sing to me. I like that.'

She began in a shaky voice.

> 'Every night at half past eight
> Comes tap tap tapping –'

'Not that one. I don't like that one. Sing *Before I was set free*.'

She sat near me and sang very softly, 'Before I was set free'. I heard as far as 'The sorrow that my heart feels for –' I didn't hear the end but I heard that before I slept, 'The sorrow that my heart feels for.'

I was going to see my mother. I had insisted that Christophine must be with me, no one else, and as I was not yet quite well they had given way. I remember the dull feeling as we drove along for I did not expect to see her. She was part of Coulibri, that had gone, so she had gone, I was certain of it. But when we reached the tidy pretty little house where she lived now (they said) I jumped out of the carriage and ran as fast as I could across the lawn. One door was open on to the veranda. I went in without knocking and stared at the people in the room. A coloured man, a coloured woman, and a white woman sitting with her head bent so low that I couldn't see her face. But I recognized her hair, one plait much shorter than the other. And her dress. I put my arms round her and kissed her. She held me so tightly that I couldn't breathe and I thought, 'It's not her.' Then, 'It must be her.' She looked at the door, then at me, then at the door again. I could not say, 'He is dead,' so I shook my head. 'But I am here, I am here,' I said, and she said, 'No,' quietly. Then 'No no no' very loudly and flung me from her. I fell against the partition and hurt myself. The man and the woman

[margin note: only recognizes physical aspects, not anything more]

[margin note: more rejection from her mother]

[margin note: would have been accepted if she was male (Pierre)]

Wide Sargasso Sea

were holding her arms and Christophine was there. The woman said, 'Why you bring the child to make <u>trouble, trouble, trouble?</u> Trouble enough without that.'

All the way back to Aunt Cora's house we didn't speak.

5   The first day I had to go to the convent, I clung to Aunt Cora as you would cling to life if you loved it. At last she got impatient, so I forced myself away from her and through the passage, down the steps into the street and, as <u>I knew they would be, they were waiting for me under the sandbox tree.</u> There were two of them, a boy and

10 a girl. The boy was about fourteen and tall and big for his age, he had a white skin, a dull ugly white covered with freckles, his mouth was a negro's mouth and he had small eyes, like bits of green glass. He had the eyes of a dead fish. Worst, most horrible of all, his hair was crinkled, a negro's hair, but bright red, and his eyebrows and

15 eyelashes were red. The girl was very black and wore no head handkerchief. Her hair had been plaited and I could smell the sickening oil she had daubed on it, from where I stood on the steps of Aunt Cora's dark, clean, friendly house, staring at them. They looked so harmless and quiet, no one would have noticed the glint

20 in the boy's eyes.

Then the girl grinned and began to crack the knuckles of her fingers. At each crack I jumped and my hands began to sweat. I was holding some school books in my right hand and I shifted them to under my arm, but it was too late, there was a mark on the palm

25 of my hand and a stain on the cover of the book. The girl began to laugh, very quietly, and it was then that hate came to me and courage with the hate so that I was able to walk past without looking at them.

I knew they were following, I knew too that as long as I was in

30 sight of Aunt Cora's house they would do nothing but stroll along some distance after me. But I knew when they would draw close. It would be when I was going up the hill. There were walls and gardens on each side of the hill and no one would be there at this hour of the morning.

35 Half-way up they closed in on me and started talking. The girl said, 'Look the crazy girl, you crazy like your mother. Your aunt

frightened to have you in the house. She send you for the nuns to lock up. Your mother walk about with no shoes and stockings on her feet, she *sans culottes*. She try to kill her husband and she try to kill you too that day you go to see her. She have eyes like zombie and you have eyes like zombie too. Why you won't look at me.' 5
The boy only said, 'One day I catch you alone, you wait, one day I catch you alone.' When I got to the top of the hill they were jostling me, I could smell the girl's hair.

A long empty street stretched away to the convent, the convent wall and a wooden gate. I would have to ring before I could get in. 10 The girl said, 'You don't want to look at me, eh, I make you look at me.' She pushed me and the books I was carrying fell to the ground.

I stooped to pick them up and saw that a tall boy who was walking along the other side of the street had stopped and looked 15 towards us. Then he crossed over, running. He had long legs, his almost feet hardly touched the ground. As soon as they saw him, they an angelic turned and walked away. He looked after them, puzzled. I would appearance have died sooner than run when they were there, but as soon as (experience) they had gone, I ran. I left one of my books on the ground and the 20 tall boy came after me.   contrast between her mother
                                                              and Mason.
'You dropped this,' he said, and smiled. I knew who he was, his name was Sandi, Alexander Cosway's son. Once I would have said 'my cousin Sandi' but Mr Mason's lectures had made me shy about my coloured relatives. I muttered, 'Thank you.' 25
'I'll talk to that boy,' he said. 'He won't bother you again.'

In the distance I could see my enemy's red hair as he pelted along, but he hadn't a chance. Sandi caught him up before he reached the corner. The girl had disappeared. I didn't wait to see what happened but I pulled and pulled at the bell. 30

At last the door opened. The nun was a coloured woman and she seemed displeased. 'You must not ring the bell like that,' she said. 'I come as quick as I can.' Then I heard the door shut behind me.

I collapsed and began to cry. She asked me if I was sick, but I 35 could not answer. She took my hand, still clicking her tongue and

muttering in an ill-tempered way, and led me across the yard, past the shadow of the big tree, not into the front door but into a big, cool, stoneflagged room. There were pots and pans hanging on the wall and a stone fireplace. There was another nun at the back of
5   the room and when the bell rang again, the first one went to answer it. The second nun, also a coloured woman, brought a basin and water but as fast as she sponged my face, so fast did I cry. When she saw my hand she asked if I had fallen and hurt myself. I shook my head and she sponged the stain away gently. 'What is the
10   matter, what are you crying about? What has happened to you?' And still I could not answer. She brought me a glass of milk, I tried to drink it, but I choked. 'Oh la la,' she said, shrugging her shoulders and went out.

When she came in again, a third nun was with her who said in a
15   calm voice, 'You have cried quite enough now, you must stop. Have you got a handkerchief?'

I remembered that I had dropped it. The new nun wiped my eyes with a large handkerchief, gave it to me and asked my name.

'Antoinette,' I said.
20   'Of course,' she said. 'I know. You are Antoinette Cosway, that is to say Antoinette Mason. Has someone frightened you?'

'Yes.'

'Now look at me,' she said. 'You will not be frightened of me.'

I looked at her. She had large brown eyes, very soft, and was
25   dressed in white, not with a starched apron like the others had. The band round her face was of linen and above the white linen a black veil of some thin material, which fell in folds down her back. Her cheeks were red, she had a laughing face and two deep dimples. Her hands were small but they looked clumsy and
30   swollen, not like the rest of her. It was only afterwards that I found out that they were crippled with rheumatism. She took me into a parlour furnished stiffly with straight-backed chairs and a polished table in the middle. After she had talked to me I told her a little of why I was crying and that I did not like walking to school
35   alone.

'That must be seen to,' she said. 'I will write to your aunt. Now

Mother St Justine will be waiting for you. I have sent for a girl who has been with us for nearly a year. Her name is Louise – Louise de Plana. If you feel strange, she will explain everything.'

Louise and I walked along a paved path to the classroom. There was grass on each side of the path and trees and shadows of trees 5 and sometimes a bright bush of flowers. She was very pretty and when she smiled at me I could scarcely believe I had ever been miserable. She said, 'We always call Mother St Justine, Mother Juice of a Lime. She is not very intelligent, poor woman. You will see.' 10

losing her ability to narrate foreshadows her losing it later

Quickly, while I can, I must remember the hot classroom. The hot classroom, the pitchpine desks, the heat of the bench striking up through my body, along my arms and hands. But outside I could see cool, blue shadow on a white wall. My needle is sticky, and creaks as it goes in and out of the canvas. 'My needle is 15 swearing,' I whisper to Louise, who sits next to me. We are cross-stitching silk roses on a pale background. We can colour the roses as we choose and mine are green, blue and purple. Underneath, I will write my name in fire red, Antoinette Mason, née Cosway, Mount Calvary Convent, Spanish Town, Jamaica, 1839. *red is the* 20 *colour of identity*

As we work, Mother St Justine reads us stories from the lives of the Saints, St Rose, St Barbara, St Agnes. But we have our own Saint, the skeleton of a girl of fourteen under the altar of the convent chapel. The Relics. But how did the nuns get them out here, I ask myself? In a cabin trunk? Specially packed for the hold? 25 How? But here she is, and St Innocenzia is her name. We do not know her story, she is not in the book. The saints we hear about were all very beautiful and wealthy. All were loved by rich and handsome young men.

'. . . more lovely and more richly dressed than he had ever seen 30 her in life,' drones Mother St Justine. 'She smiled and said, "Here Theophilus is a rose from the garden of my Spouse, in whom you did not believe." The rose he found by his side when he awoke has never faded. It still exists.' (Oh, but where? Where?) 'And Theophilus was converted to Christianity,' says Mother St Justine, 35

reading very rapidly now, 'and became one of the Holy Martyrs.'
She shuts the book with a clap and talks about pushing down the
cuticles of our nails when we wash our hands. Cleanliness, good
manners and kindness to God's poor. A flow of words. ('It is her
5 time of life,' said Hélène de Plana, 'she cannot help it, poor old
Justine.') 'When you insult or injure the unfortunate or the
unhappy, you insult Christ Himself and He will not forget, for
they are His chosen ones.' This remark is made in a casual and
perfunctory voice and she slides on to order and chastity, that
10 flawless crystal that, once broken, can never be mended. Also
deportment. Like everyone else, she has fallen under the spell of
the de Plana sisters and holds them up as an example to the class.
I admire them. They sit so poised and imperturbable while she
points out the excellence of Miss Hélène's coiffure, achieved with-
15 out a looking-glass. *making herself acceptable without seeing her identity, her alter ego*

'Please, Hélène, tell me how you do your hair, because when I
grow up I want mine to look like yours.'

'It's very easy. You comb it upwards, like this and then push it
a little forward, like that, and then you pin it here and here. Never
20 too many pins.'

'Yes, but Hélène, mine does not look like yours, whatever I do.'

Her eyelashes flickered, she turned away, too polite to say the
obvious thing. We have no looking-glass in the dormitory, once I
saw the new young nun from Ireland looking at herself in a cask of
25 water, smiling to see if her dimples were still there. When she
noticed me, she blushed and I thought, now she will always dislike
me.

Sometimes it was Miss Hélène's hair and sometimes Miss Germaine's impeccable deportment, and sometimes it was the care
30 Miss Louise took of her beautiful teeth. And if we were never
envious, they never seemed vain. Hélène and Germaine, a little
disdainful, aloof perhaps, but Louise, not even that. She took no
part in it – as if she knew that she was born for other things. Hélène's
brown eyes could snap, Germaine's grey eyes were beautiful, soft
35 and cow-like, she spoke slowly and, unlike most Creole girls, was
very even-tempered. It is easy to imagine what happened to those

two, bar accidents. Ah but Louise ! Her small waist, her thin brown hands, her black curls which smelled of vetiver, her high sweet voice, singing so carelessly in Chapel about death. Like a bird would sing. Anything might have happened to you, Louise, anything at all, and I wouldn't be surprised.   5

Then there was another saint, said Mother St Justine, she lived later on but still in Italy, or was it in Spain. Italy is white pillars and green water. Spain is hot sun on stones. France is a lady with black hair wearing a white dress because Louise was born in France fifteen years ago, and my mother, whom I must forget and pray for   10 as though she were dead, though she is living, liked to dress in white.

No one spoke of her now that Christophine had left us to live with her son. I seldom saw my stepfather. He seemed to dislike Jamaica, Spanish Town in particular, and was often away for   15 months.

One hot afternoon in July my aunt told me that she was going to England for a year. Her health was not good and she needed a change. As she talked she was working at a patchwork counterpane. The diamond-shaped pieces of silk melted one into the other, red, 20 blue, purple, green, yellow, all one shimmering colour. Hours and hours she had spent on it and it was nearly finished. Would I be lonely? she asked and I said 'No', looking at the colours. Hours and hours and hours I thought.

recognizes life and death in an instant

INSIDE = SAFE AND SECURE

This convent was my refuge, a place of sunshine and of death 25 where very early in the morning the clap of a wooden signal woke the nine of us who slept in the long dormitory. We woke to see Sister Marie Augustine sitting, serene and neat, bolt upright in a wooden chair. The long brown room was full of gold sunlight and shadows of trees moving quietly. I learnt to say very quickly as the 30 others did, 'offer up all the prayers, works and sufferings of this day.' But what about happiness, I thought at first, is there no happiness? There must be. Oh happiness of course, happiness, well.

But I soon forgot about happiness, running down the stairs to   35

the big stone bath where we splashed about wearing long grey cotton chemises which reached to our ankles. The smell of soap as you cautiously soaped yourself under the chemise, a trick to be learned, dressing with modesty, another trick. Great splashes of
5 sunlight as we ran up the wooden steps of the refectory. Hot coffee and rolls and melting butter. But after the meal, now and at the hour of our death, and at midday and at six in the evening, now and at the hour of our death. Let perpetual light shine on them. This is for my mother, I would think, wherever her soul is wandering, for
10 it has left her body. Then I remembered how she hated a strong light and loved the cool and the shade. It is a different light they told me. Still, I would not say it. Soon we were back in the shifting shadows outside, more beautiful than any perpetual light could be, and soon I learnt to gabble without thinking as the others did.
15 About changing now and the hour of our death for that is all we have.

Everything was brightness, or dark. The walls, the blazing colours of the flowers in the garden, the nuns' habits were bright, but their veils, the Crucifix hanging from their waists, the shadow
20 of the trees, were black. That was how it was, light and dark, sun and shadow, Heaven and Hell, for one of the nuns knew all about Hell and who does not? But another one knew about Heaven and the attributes of the blessed, of which the least is transcendent beauty. The very least. I could hardly wait for all this ecstasy and
25 once I prayed for a long time to be dead. Then remembered that this was a sin. It's presumption or despair, I forget which, but a mortal sin. So I prayed for a long time about that too, but the thought came, so many things are sins, why? Another sin, to think that. However, happily, Sister Marie Augustine says thoughts are
30 not sins, if they are driven away at once. You say Lord save me, I perish. I find it very comforting to know exactly what must be done. All the same, I did not pray so often after that and soon, hardly at all. I felt bolder, happier, more free. But not so safe.

During this time, nearly eighteen months, my stepfather often
35 came to see me. He interviewed Mother Superior first, then I would go into the parlour dressed ready for a dinner or a visit to friends. He

Mason relys on another
perspective of her before
seeing her true identity

gave me presents when we parted, sweets, a locket, a bracelet, once a very pretty dress which, of course, I could not wear.

The last time he came was different. I knew that as soon as I got into the room. He kissed me, held me at arm's length looking at me carefully and critically, then smiled and said that I was taller 5 than he thought. I reminded him that I was over seventeen, a grown woman. 'I've not forgotten your present,' he said.

Because I felt shy and ill at ease I answered coldly, 'I can't wear all these things you buy for me.'

'You can wear what you like when you live with me,' he said. 10

'Where? In Trinidad?'

'Of course not. Here, for the time being. With me and your Aunt Cora who is coming home at last. She says another English winter will kill her. And Richard. You can't be hidden away all your life.' 15

'Why not?' I thought.

I suppose he noticed my dismay because he began to joke, pay me compliments, and ask me such absurd questions that soon I was laughing too. How would I like to live in England? Then, before I could answer, had I learnt dancing, or were the nuns too 20 strict?

'They are not strict at all,' I said. 'The Bishop who visits them every year says they are lax. Very lax. It's the climate he says.'

'I hope they told him to mind his own business.'

'She did. Mother Superior did. Some of the others were fright- 25 ened. They are not strict but no one has taught me to dance.'

'That won't be the difficulty. I want you to be happy, Antoinette, secure, I've tried to arrange it, but we'll have time to talk about that later.'

As we were going out of the convent gate he said in a careless 30 voice, 'I have asked some English friends to spend next winter here. You won't be dull.'

'Do you think they'll come?' I said doubtfully.

'One of them will. I'm certain of that.'

It may have been the way he smiled, but again a feeling of dismay, 35 sadness, loss, almost choked me. This time I did not let him see it.

33

It was like that morning when I found the dead horse. Say nothing and it may not be true.

But they all knew at the convent. The girls were very curious but I would not answer their questions and for the first time I resented
5　the nuns' cheerful faces.

They are safe. How can they know what it can be like *outside*? This was the second time I had my dream. FORESHADOWING Again I have left the house at Coulibri. It is still night and I am walking towards the forest. I am wearing a long dress and thin
10　slippers, so I walk with difficulty, following the man who is with me and holding up the skirt of my dress. It is white and beautiful and I don't wish to get it soiled. I follow him, sick with fear but I make no effort to save myself; if anyone were to try to save me, I would refuse. This must happen. Now we have reached the forest.
15　We are under the tall dark trees and there is no wind. 'Here?' He turns and looks at me, his face black with hatred, and when I see this I begin to cry. He smiles slyly. 'Not here, not yet,' he says, and I follow him, weeping. Now I do not try to hold up my dress, it trails in the dirt, my beautiful dress. We are no longer in the forest
20　but in an enclosed garden surrounded by a stone wall and the trees are different trees. I do not know them. There are steps leading upwards. It is too dark to see the wall or the steps, but I know they are there and I think, 'It will be when I go up these steps. At the top.' I stumble over my dress and cannot get up. I touch a tree and
25　my arms hold on to it. 'Here, here.' But I think I will not go any further. The tree sways and jerks as if it is trying to throw me off. Still I cling and the seconds pass and each one is a thousand years. 'Here, in here,' a strange voice said, and the tree stopped swaying and jerking.

30　Now Sister Marie Augustine is leading me out of the dormitory, asking if I am ill, telling me that I must not disturb the others and though I am still shivering I wonder if she will take me behind the mysterious curtains to the place where she sleeps. But no. She seats me in a chair, vanishes, and after a while comes back with a cup of
35　hot chocolate.

34

I said, 'I dreamed I was in Hell.'

'That dream is evil. Put it from your mind – never think of it again,' and she rubbed my cold hands to warm them.

She looks as usual, composed and neat, and I want to ask her if she gets up before dawn or hasn't been to bed at all.

'Drink your chocolate.'

While I am drinking it I remember that after my mother's funeral, very early in the morning, almost as early as this, we went home to drink chocolate and eat cakes. She died last year, no one told me how, and I didn't ask. Mr Mason was there and Christophine, no one else. Christophine cried bitterly but I could not. I prayed, but the words fell to the ground meaning nothing.

Now the thought of her is mixed up with my dream.

I saw her in her mended habit riding a borrowed horse, trying to wave at the head of the cobblestoned road at Coulibri, and tears came to my eyes again. 'Such terrible things happen,' I said. 'Why? Why?'

'You must not concern yourself with that mystery,' said Sister Maria Augustine. 'We do not know why the devil must have his little day. Not yet.'

She never smiled as much as the others, now she was not smiling at all. She looked sad.

She said, as if she was talking to herself, 'Now go quietly back to bed. Think of calm, peaceful things and try to sleep. Soon I will give the signal. Soon it will be tomorrow morning.'

Time, character and reality are shattered.

Part Two

war diction
contrasting ironically with what
should be a happy post-marriage mood

So it was all over, the advance and retreat, the doubts and hesita-
tions. Everything finished, for better or for worse. There we were,
sheltering from the heavy rain under a large mango tree, myself,
my wife Antoinette and a little half-caste servant who was called
5 Amélie. Under a neighbouring tree I could see our luggage covered
with sacking, the two porters and a boy holding fresh horses, hired
to carry us up 2,000 feet to the waiting honeymoon house.

The girl Amélie said this morning, 'I hope you will be very happy,
sir, in your sweet honeymoon house.' She was laughing at me I
10 could see. A lovely little creature but sly, spiteful, malignant
perhaps, like much else in this place. *Foreshadows Rochester's*
relationship with her.
'It's only a shower,' Antoinette said anxiously. 'It will soon stop.'

I looked at the sad leaning coconut palms, the fishing boats
drawn up on the shingly beach, the uneven row of whitewashed
15 huts, and asked the name of the village.

'Massacre.'

'And who was massacred here? Slaves?'

'Oh no.' She sounded shocked. 'Not slaves. Something must
have happened a long time ago. Nobody remembers now.'

20 The rain fell more heavily, huge drops sounded like hail on
the leaves of the tree, and the sea crept stealthily forwards and
backwards.

So this is Massacre. Not the end of the world, only the last stage
of our interminable journey from Jamaica, the start of our sweet
25 honeymoon. And it will all look very different in the sun.

It had been arranged that we would leave Spanish Town immediately after the ceremony and spend some weeks in one of the

*sympathy given because
he gives up control of his fate.*

Windward Islands, at a small estate which had belonged to Antoinette's mother. I agreed. As I had agreed to everything else.

The windows of the huts were shut, the doors opened into silence and dimness. Then three little boys came to stare at us. The smallest wore nothing but a religious medal round his neck and 5
the brim of a large fisherman's hat. When I smiled at him, he began to cry. A woman called from one of the huts and he ran away, still howling.

The other two followed slowly, looking back several times.

As if this was a signal a second woman appeared at her door, 10
then a third.

'It's Caro,' Antoinette said. 'I'm sure it's Caro. Caroline,' she called, waving, and the woman waved back. A gaudy old creature in a brightly flowered dress, a striped head handkerchief and gold ear-rings. 15

'You'll get soaked, Antoinette,' I said.

'No, the rain is stopping.' She held up the skirt of her riding habit and ran across the street. I watched her critically. She wore a tricorne hat which became her. At least it shadowed her eyes which are too large and can be disconcerting. She never blinks at 20
all it seems to me. Long, sad, dark alien eyes. Creole of pure English descent she may be, but they are not English or European either. And when did I begin to notice all this about my wife Antoinette? After we left Spanish Town I suppose. Or did I notice it before and refuse to admit what I saw? Not that I had much time 25
to notice anything. I was married a month after I arrived in Jamaica and for nearly three weeks of that time I was in bed with fever.

The two women stood in the doorway of the hut gesticulating, talking not English but the debased French patois they use in this island. The rain began to drip down the back of my neck adding 30
to my feeling of discomfort and melancholy.

I thought about the letter which should have been written to England a week ago. Dear Father . . .

'Caroline asks if you will shelter in her house.'

This was Antoinette. She spoke hesitatingly as if she expected 35
me to refuse, so it was easy to do so.

'But you are getting wet,' she said.

'I don't mind that.' I smiled at Caroline and shook my head.

'She will be very disappointed,' said my wife, crossed the street again and went into the dark hut.

5   Amélie, who had been sitting with her back to us, turned round. Her expression was so full of delighted malice, so intelligent, above all so intimate that I felt ashamed and looked away.

'Well,' I thought. 'I have had fever. I am not myself yet.'

The rain was not so heavy and I went to talk to the porters. The
10 first man was not a native of the island. 'This a very wild place – not civilized. Why you come here?' He was called the Young Bull he told me, and he was twenty-seven years of age. A magnificent body and a foolish conceited face. The other man's name was Emile, yes, he was born in the village, he lived there. 'Ask him how
15 old he is,' suggested the Young Bull. Emile said in a questioning voice, 'Fourteen? Yes I have fourteen years master.'

'Impossible,' I said. I could see the grey hairs in his sparse beard.

'Fifty-six years perhaps.' He seemed anxious to please.

The Young Bull laughed loudly. 'He don't know how old he is,
20 he don't think about it. I tell you sir these people are not civilized.'

Emile muttered, 'My mother she know, but she dead.' Then he produced a blue rag which he twisted into a pad and put on his head.

Most of the women were outside their doors looking at us but
25 without smiling. Sombre people in a sombre place. Some of the men were going to their boats. When Emile shouted, two of them came towards him. He sang in a deep voice. They answered, then lifted the heavy wicker basket and swung it on to his head-pad singing. He tested the balance with one hand and strode off,
30 barefooted on the sharp stones, by far the gayest member of the wedding party. As the Young Bull was loaded up he glanced at me sideways boastfully and he too sang to himself in English.

The boy brought the horses to a large stone and I saw Antoinette coming from the hut. The sun blazed out and steam rose from the
35 green behind us. Amélie took her shoes off, tied them together and hung them round her neck. She balanced her small basket on her

→ // to Daniel

head and swung away as easily as the porters. We mounted, turned
a corner and the village was out of sight. A cock crowed loudly and
I remembered the night before which we had spent in the town.
Antoinette had a room to herself, she was exhausted. I lay awake
listening to cocks crowing all night, then got up very early and saw   5
the women with trays covered with white cloths on their heads
going to the kitchen. The woman with small hot loaves for sale,
the woman with cakes, the woman with sweets. In the street another
called *Bon sirop, Bon sirop,* and I felt peaceful.

positive connotation

The road climbed upward. On one side the wall of green, on the   10
other a steep drop to the ravine below. We pulled up and looked
at the hills, the mountains and the blue-green sea. There was a soft
warm wind blowing but I understood why the porter had called it
a wild place. Not only wild but menacing. Those hills would close
in on you.   15

'What an extreme green,' was all I could say, and thinking of
Emile calling to the fishermen and the sound of his voice, I asked
about him.

'They take short cuts. They will be at Granbois long before we
are.' gives identity to Antoinette but Rochester thinks its TOO INTENSE   20

Everything is too much, I felt as I rode wearily after her. Too
much blue, too much purple, too much green. The flowers too
red, the mountains too high, the hills too near. And the woman is
a stranger. Her pleading expression annoys me. I have not bought
her, she has bought me, or so she thinks. I looked down at the   25
coarse mane of the horse . . . Dear Father. The thirty thousand
pounds have been paid to me without question or condition. No
provision made for her (that must be seen to). I have a modest
competence now. I will never be a disgrace to you or to my dear
brother the son you love. No begging letters, no mean requests.   30
None of the furtive shabby manoeuvres of a younger son. I have
sold my soul or you have sold it, and after all is it such a bad
bargain? The girl is thought to be beautiful, she is beautiful. And
yet . . .

Meanwhile the horses jogged along a very bad road. It was   35 getting cooler. A bird whistled, a long sad note. 'What bird is that?' She was too far ahead and did not hear me. The bird whistled again. A mountain bird. Shrill and sweet. A very lonely sound.

She stopped and called, 'Put your coat on now.' I did so and
5 realized that I was no longer pleasantly cool but cold in my sweat-soaked shirt.

We rode on again, silent in the slanting afternoon sun, the wall of trees on one side, a drop on the other. Now the sea was a serene blue, deep and dark.

10 We came to a little river. 'This is the boundary of Granbois.' She smiled at me. It was the first time I had seen her smile simply and naturally. Or perhaps it was the first time I had felt simple and natural with her. A bamboo spout jutted from the cliff, the water coming from it was silver blue. She dismounted quickly, picked a
15 large shamrock-shaped leaf to make a cup, and drank. Then she picked another leaf, folded it and brought it to me. 'Taste. This is mountain water.' Looking up smiling, she might have been any pretty English girl and to please her I drank. It was cold, pure and sweet, a beautiful colour against the thick green leaf.

20 She said, 'After this we go down then up again. Then we are there.'

Next time she spoke she said, 'The earth is red here, do you notice?'

'It's red in parts of England too.'

25 'Oh England, England,' she called back mockingly, and the sound went on and on like a warning I did not choose to hear.

Soon the road was cobblestoned and we stopped at a flight of stone steps. There was a large screw pine to the left and to the right what looked like an imitation of an English summer house – four
30 wooden posts and a thatched roof. She dismounted and ran up the steps. At the top a badly cut, coarse-grained lawn and at the end of the lawn a shabby white house. 'Now you are at Granbois.' I looked at the mountains purple against a very blue sky.

Perched up on wooden stilts the house seemed to shrink from
35 the forest behind it and crane eagerly out to the distant sea. It was more awkward than ugly, a little sad as if it knew it could not last.

A group of negroes were standing at the foot of the veranda steps. Antoinette ran across the lawn and as I followed her I collided with a boy coming in the opposite direction. He rolled his eyes, looking alarmed and went on towards the horses without a word of apology. A man's voice said, 'Double up now double up. Look sharp.' There were four of them. A woman, a girl and a tall, dignified man were together. Antoinette was standing with her arms round another woman. 'That was Bertrand who nearly knocked you down. That is Rose and Hilda. This is Baptiste.'

The servants grinned shyly as she named them.

'And here is Christophine who was my da, my nurse long ago.'

Baptiste said that it was a happy day and that we'd brought fine weather with us. He spoke good English, but in the middle of his address of welcome Hilda began to giggle. She was a young girl of about twelve or fourteen, wearing a sleeveless white dress which just reached her knees. The dress was spotless but her uncovered hair, though it was oiled and braided into many small plaits, gave her a savage appearance. Baptiste frowned at her and she giggled more loudly, then put her hand over her mouth and went up the wooden steps into the house. I could hear her bare feet running along the veranda.

'*Doudou, ché cocotte*,' the elderly woman said to Antoinette. I looked at her sharply but she seemed insignificant. She was blacker than most and her clothes, even the handkerchief round her head, were subdued in colour. She looked at me steadily, not with approval, I thought. We stared at each other for quite a minute. I looked away first and she smiled to herself, gave Antoinette a little push forward and disappeared into the shadows at the back of the house. The other servants had gone.

Standing on the veranda I breathed the sweetness of the air. Cloves I could smell and cinnamon, roses and orange blossom. And an intoxicating freshness as if all this had never been breathed before. When Antoinette said 'Come, I will show you the house' I went with her unwillingly for the rest of the place seemed neglected and deserted. She led me into a large unpainted room. There was a small shabby sofa, a mahogany table in the middle, some straight-backed chairs and an old oak chest with brass feet like lion's claws.

Holding my hand she went up to the sideboard where two glasses of rum punch were waiting for us. She handed me one and said, 5 'To happiness.' NOT HAPPY

'To happiness,' I answered. > can't elaborate on being happy

The room beyond was larger and emptier. There were two doors, one leading to the veranda, the other very slightly open into a small room. A big bed, a round table by its side, two chairs, a surprising 10 dressing-table with a marble top and a large looking-glass. Two wreaths of frangipani lay on the bed.

'Am I expected to wear one of these? And when?'

I crowned myself with one of the wreaths and made a face in the glass. 'I hardly think it suits my handsome face, do you?'

15 'You look like a king, an emperor.'

'God forbid,' I said and took the wreath off. It fell on the floor and as I went towards the window I stepped on it. The room was full of the scent of crushed flowers. I saw her reflection in the glass fanning herself with a small palm-leaf fan coloured blue and red at 20 the edges. I felt sweat on my forehead and sat down, she knelt near me and wiped my face with her handkerchief.

'Don't you like it here? This is my place and everything is on our side. Once,' she said, 'I used to sleep with a piece of wood by my side so that I could defend myself if I were attacked. That's how 25 afraid I was.'

'Afraid of what?'

She shook her head. 'Of nothing, of everything.'

Someone knocked and she said, 'It's only Christophine.'

'The old woman who was your nurse? Are you afraid of her?'

30 'No, how could I be?'

'If she were taller,' I said, 'one of these strapping women dressed up to the nines, I might be afraid of her.'

She laughed. 'That door leads into your dressing-room.'

I shut it gently after me.

35 It seemed crowded after the emptiness of the rest of the house. There was a carpet, the only one I had seen, a press made of some

beautiful wood I did not recognize. Under the open window a small writing-desk with paper, pens, and ink. 'A refuge' I was thinking when someone said, 'This was Mr Mason's room, sir, but he did not come here often. He did not like the place.' Baptiste, standing in the doorway to the veranda, had a blanket over his arm.   5

'It's all very comfortable,' I said. He laid the blanket on the bed.

'It can be cold here at night,' he said. Then went away. But the feeling of security had left me. I looked round suspiciously. The door into her room could be bolted, a stout wooden bar pushed across the other. This was the last room in the house. Wooden   10
steps from the veranda led on to another rough lawn, a Seville orange tree grew by the steps. I went back into the dressing-room and looked out of the window. I saw a clay road, muddy in places, bordered by a row of tall trees. Beyond the road various half-hidden outbuildings. One was the kitchen. No chimney but smoke was   15
pouring out of the window. I sat on the soft narrow bed and listened. Not a sound except the river. I might have been alone in the house. There was a crude bookshelf made of three shingles strung together over the desk and I looked at the books, Byron's poems, novels by Sir Walter Scott, *Confessions of an Opium Eater*,   20
some shabby brown volumes, and on the last shelf, <u>*Life and Letters of* . . .</u> The rest was eaten away. ▷ suggestion of decay, in this setting always something good with something bad. PARADOXICAL

Dear Father, we have arrived from Jamaica after an uncomfortable few days. This little estate in the Windward Islands is part of the family property and Antoinette is much attached to it. She wished to get here as soon as   25
possible. All is well and has gone according to your plans and wishes. I dealt of course with Richard Mason. His father died soon after I left for the West Indies as you probably know. He is a good fellow, hospitable and friendly; he seemed to become attached to me and trusted me completely. This place is very beautiful but my illness has left me too exhausted to   30
appreciate it fully. I will write again in a few days' time.

I reread this letter and added a postscript:

I feel that I have left you too long without news for the bare announcement of my approaching marriage was hardly news. I was down with fever for

two weeks after I got to Spanish Town. Nothing serious but I felt wretched enough. I stayed with the Frasers, friends of the Masons. Mr Fraser is an Englishman, a retired magistrate, and he insisted on telling me at length about some of his cases. It was difficult to think or write coherently. In this
5 cool and remote place it is called Granbois (the High Woods I suppose) I feel better already and my next letter will be longer and more explicit.

A cool and remote place . . . And I wondered how they got their letters posted. I folded mine and put it into a drawer of the desk.

As for my confused impressions they will never be written. There
10 are blanks in my mind that cannot be filled up.

*indefinite pronoun means
it is foreign, unknown to him.*

It was all very brightly coloured, very strange, but it meant nothing to me. Nor did she, the girl I was to marry. When at last I met her I bowed, smiled, kissed her hand, danced with her. I played the part I was expected to play. She never had anything to do with me
15 at all. Every movement I made was an effort of will and sometimes I wondered that no one noticed this. I would listen to my own voice and marvel at it, calm, correct but toneless, surely. But I must have given a faultless performance. If I saw an expression of doubt or curiosity it was on a black face not a white one.
20   I remember little of the actual ceremony. Marble memorial tablets on the walls commemorating the virtues of the last genera-tion of planters. All benevolent. All slave-owners. All resting in peace. When we came out of the church I took her hand. It was cold as ice in the hot sun.
25   Then I was at a long table in a crowded room. Palm leaf fans, a mob of servants, the women's head handkerchiefs striped red and yellow, the men's dark faces. The strong taste of punch, the cleaner taste of champagne, my bride in white but I hardly remember what she looked like. Then in another room women dressed in black.
30 Cousin Julia, Cousin Ada, Aunt Lina. Thin or fat they all looked alike. Gold ear-rings in pierced ears. Silver bracelets jangling on their wrists. I said to one of them, 'We are leaving Jamaica tonight,' and she answered after a pause, 'Of course, Antoinette does not

like Spanish Town. Nor did her mother.' Peering at me. (Do
their eyes get smaller as they grow older? Smaller, beadier, more
inquisitive?) After that I thought I saw the same expression on all
their faces. Curiosity? Pity? Ridicule? But why should they pity me.
I who have done so well for myself?   5

The morning before the wedding Richard Mason burst into my
room at the Frasers as I was finishing my first cup of coffee. 'She
won't go through with it!'

'Won't go through with what?'

'She won't marry you.'   10

'But why?'

'She doesn't say why.'

'She must have some reason.'

'She won't give a reason. I've been arguing with the little fool
for an hour.'   15

We stared at each other.

'Everything arranged, the presents, the invitations. What shall I
tell your father?' He seemed on the verge of tears.

I said, 'If she won't, she won't. She can't be dragged to the altar.
Let me get dressed. I must hear what she has to say.'   20

He went out meekly and while I dressed I thought that this
would indeed make a fool of me. I did not relish going back to
England in the role of rejected suitor jilted by this Creole girl. I
must certainly know why.

She was sitting in a rocking chair with her head bent. Her hair   25
was in two long plaits over her shoulders. From a little distance I
spoke gently. 'What is the matter, Antoinette? What have I done?'
She said nothing.

'You don't wish to marry me?'

'No.' She spoke in a very low voice.   30

'But why?'

'I'm afraid of what may happen.'

'But don't you remember last night I told you that when you are
my wife there would not be any more reason to be afraid?'

'Yes,' she said. 'Then Richard came in and you laughed. I didn't 35
like the way you laughed.'

LIE
he already
distrusts
her.

'But I was laughing at myself, Antoinette.'

She looked at me and I took her in my arms and kissed her.

'You don't know anything about me,' she said.

'I'll trust you if you'll trust me. Is that a bargain? You will make
5 me very unhappy if you send me away without telling me what I
have done to displease you. I will go with a sad heart.'

'Your sad heart,' she said, and touched my face. I kissed her
fervently, promising her peace, happiness, safety, but when I said,
'Can I tell poor Richard that it was a mistake? He is sad too,' she
10 did not answer me. Only nodded.

*

Thinking of all this, of Richard's angry face, her voice saying, 'Can
you give me peace?', I must have slept.

I woke to the sound of voices in the next room, laughter and
water being poured out. I listened, still drowsy. Antoinette said,
15 'Don't put any more scent on my hair. He doesn't like it.' The
other: 'The man don't like scent? I never hear that before.' It was
almost dark.

The dining-room was brilliantly lit. Candles on the table, a row
on the sideboard, three-branch candlesticks on the old sea-chest.
20 The two doors on to the veranda stood open but there was no
wind. The flames burned straight. She was sitting on the sofa and
I wondered why I had never realized how beautiful she was. Her
hair was combed away from her face and fell smoothly far below
her waist. I could see the red and gold lights in it. She seemed
25 pleased when I complimented her on her dress and told me she
had it made in St Pierre, Martinique. 'They call this fashion *à la
Joséphine.*'

'You talk of St Pierre as though it were Paris,' I said.

'But it is the Paris of the West Indies.'

30 There were trailing pink flowers on the table and the name
echoed pleasantly in my head. Coralita Coralita. The food, though
too highly seasoned, was lighter and more appetizing than anything
I had tasted in Jamaica. We drank champagne. A great many moths
and beetles found their way into the room, flew into the candles

and fell dead on the tablecloth. Amélie swept them up with a crumb brush. Uselessly. More moths and beetles came.

'Is it true,' she said, 'that England is like a dream? Because one of my friends who married an Englishman wrote and told me so. She said this place London is like a cold dark dream sometimes. I want to wake up.'

'Well,' I answered annoyed, 'that is precisely how your beautiful island seems to me, quite unreal and like a dream.'

'But how can rivers and mountains and the sea be unreal?'

'And how can millions of people, their houses and their streets be unreal?'

'More easily,' she said, 'much more easily. Yes a big city must be like a dream.'

'No, this is unreal and like a dream,' I thought.

The long veranda was furnished with canvas chairs, two hammocks, and a wooden table on which stood a tripod telescope. Amélie brought out candles with glass shades but the night swallowed up the feeble light. There was a very strong scent of flowers – the flowers by the river that open at night she told me – and the noise, subdued in the inner room, was deafening. 'Crac-cracs,' she explained, 'they make a sound like their name, and crickets and frogs.'

I leaned on the railing and saw hundreds of fireflies – 'Ah yes, fireflies in Jamaica, here they call a firefly La belle.'

A large moth, so large that I thought it was a bird, blundered into one of the candles, put it out and fell to the floor. 'He's a big fellow,' I said.

'Is it badly burned?'

'More stunned than hurt.'

I took the beautiful creature up in my handkerchief and put it on the railing. For a moment it was still and by the dim candlelight I could see the soft brilliant colours, the intricate pattern on the wings. I shook the handkerchief gently and it flew away.

'I hope that gay gentleman will be safe,' I said.

'He will come back if we don't put the candles out. It's light enough by the stars.'

Indeed the starlight was so bright that shadows of the veranda posts and the trees outside lay on the floor.

'Now come for a walk,' she said, 'and I will tell you a story.'

We walked along the veranda to the steps which led to the lawn.

'We used to come here to get away from the hot weather in June, July and August. I came three times with my Aunt Cora who is ill. That was after . . .' She stopped and put her hand up to her head.

'If this is a sad story, don't tell it to me tonight.'

'It is not sad,' she said. 'Only some things happen and are there for always even though you forget why or when. It was in that little bedroom.'

I looked where she was pointing but could only see the outline of a narrow bed and one or two chairs.

'This night I can remember it was very hot. The window was shut but I asked Christophine to open it because the breeze comes from the hills at night. The land breeze. Not from the sea. It was so hot that my night chemise was sticking to me but I went to sleep all the same. And then suddenly I was awake. I saw two enormous rats, as big as cats, on the sill staring at me.'

'I'm not astonished that you were frightened.'

'But I was not frightened. That was the strange thing. I stared at them and they did not move. I could see myself in the looking-glass the other side of the room, in my white chemise with a frill round the neck, staring at those rats and the rats quite still, staring at me.'

'Well, what happened?'

'I turned over, pulled up the sheet and went to sleep instantly.'

'And is that the story?'

'No, I woke up again suddenly like the first time and the rats were not there but I felt very frightened. I got out of bed quickly and ran on to the veranda. I lay down in this hammock. This one.' She pointed to a flat hammock, a rope at each of the four corners.

'There was a full moon that night – and I watched it for a long time. There were no clouds chasing it, so it seemed to be standing still and it shone on me. Next morning Christophine was angry. She said that it was very bad to sleep in the moonlight when the moon is full.'

[margin note, left side:] Used as a symbol of confrontation with one's self. because she doesn't know who it is she sees in the mirror.

[margin note, bottom:] opposite to Jane Eyre
Moon imagery = bad.

'And did you tell her about the rats?'

'No, I never told anyone till now. But I have never forgotten them.'

I wanted to say something reassuring but the scent of the river flowers was overpoweringly strong. I felt giddy. 5

'Do you think that too,' she said, 'that I have slept too long in the moonlight?'

Her mouth was set in a fixed smile but her eyes were so withdrawn and lonely that I put my arms round her, rocked her like a child and sang to her. An old song I thought I had forgotten: 10

> 'Hail to the queen of the silent night,
> Shine bright, shine bright Robin as you die.'

She listened, then sang with me:

> 'Shine bright, shine bright Robin as you die.'

There was no one in the house and only two candles in the room 15 which had been so brilliantly lit. Her room was dim, with a shaded candle by the bed and another on the dressing-table. There was a bottle of wine on the round table. It was very late when I poured out two glasses and told her to drink to our happiness, to our love and the day without end which would be tomorrow. I was young 20 then. A short youth mine was.

I woke next morning in the green-yellow light, feeling uneasy as though someone were watching me. She must have been awake for some time. Her hair was plaited and she wore a fresh white chemise. I turned to take her in my arms, I meant to undo the careful plaits, 25 but as I did so there was a soft discreet knock.

She said, 'I have sent Christophine away twice. We wake very early here. The morning is the best time.'

'Come in,' she called and Christophine came in with our coffee on a tray. She was dressed up and looking very imposing. The skirt 30 of her flowered dress trailed after her making a rustling noise as she walked and her yellow silk turban was elaborately tied. Long heavy gold ear-rings pulled down the lobes of her ears. She wished

Wide Sargasso Sea

us good morning smiling and put the tray of coffee, cassava cakes and guava jelly on the round table. I got out of bed and went into the dressing-room. Someone had laid my dressing-gown on the narrow bed. I looked out of the window. The cloudless sky was a
5 paler blue than I'd imagined but as I looked I thought I saw the colour changing to a deeper blue. At noon I knew it would be gold, then brassy in the heat. Now it was fresh and cool and the air itself was blue. At last I turned away from the light and space and went back into the bedroom, which was still in the half dark. Antoinette
10 was leaning back against the pillows with her eyes closed. She opened them and smiled when I came in. It was the black woman hovering over her who said, 'Taste my bull's blood, master.' The coffee she handed me was delicious and she had long-fingered hands, thin and beautiful I suppose.

15   'Not horse piss like the English madams drink,' she said. 'I know them. Drink, drink their yellow horse piss, talk, talk their lying talk.' Her dress trailed and rustled as she walked to the door. There she turned. 'I send the girl to clear up the mess you make with the frangipani, it bring cockroach in the house. Take care
20 not to slip on the flowers, young master.' She slid through the door.

   'Her coffee is delicious but her language is horrible and she might hold her dress up. It must get very dirty, yards of it trailing on the floor.'

25   'When they don't hold their dress up it's for respect,' said Antoinette. 'Or for feast days or going to Mass.'

   'And is this a feast day?'

   'She wanted it to be a feast day.'

   'Whatever the reason it is not a clean habit.'

30   'It is. You don't understand at all. They don't care about getting a dress dirty because it shows it isn't the only dress they have. Don't you like Christophine?'

   'She is a very worthy person no doubt. I can't say I like her language.'

35   'It doesn't mean anything,' said Antoinette.

   'And she looks so lazy. She dawdles about.'

50

'Again you are mistaken. She seems slow, but every move she makes is right so it's quick in the end.'

I drank another cup of bull's blood. (Bull's blood, I thought. The Young Bull.)

'How did you get that dressing-table up here?' 5

'I don't know. It's always been here ever since I can remember. A lot of the furniture was stolen, but not that.'

There were two pink roses on the tray, each in a small brown jug. One was full blown and as I touched it the petals dropped.

'*Rose elle a vécu*,' I said and laughed. 'Is that poem true? Have all 10 beautiful things sad destinies?'

'No, of course not.'

Her little fan was on the table, she took it up laughing, lay back and shut her eyes. 'I think I won't get up this morning.'

'Not get up. Not get up at all?' 15

'I'll get up when I wish to. I'm very lazy you know. Like Christophine. I often stay in bed all day.' She flourished her fan. 'The bathing pool is quite near. Go before it gets hot, Baptiste will show you. There are two pools, one we call the champagne pool because it has a waterfall, not a big one you understand, but it's 20 good to feel it on your shoulders. Underneath is the nutmeg pool, that's brown and shaded by a big nutmeg tree. It's just big enough to swim in. But be careful. Remember to put your clothes on a rock and before you dress again shake them very well. Look for the red ant, that is the worst. It is very small but bright red so you will 25 be able to see it easily if you look. Be careful,' she said and waved her little fan.

One morning soon after we arrived, the row of tall trees outside my window was covered with small pale flowers too fragile to resist the wind. They fell in a day, and looked like snow on the 30 rough grass – snow with a faint sweet scent. Then they were blown away.

The fine weather lasted longer. It lasted all that week and the next and the next and the next. No sign of a break. My fever weakness left me, so did all misgiving. 35

I went very early to the bathing pool and stayed there for hours, unwilling to leave the river, the trees shading it, the flowers that opened at night. They were tightly shut, drooping, sheltering from the sun under their thick leaves.

5 It was a beautiful place – wild, untouched, above all untouched, with an alien, disturbing, secret loveliness. And it kept its secret. I'd find myself thinking, 'What I see is nothing – I want what it *hides* – that is not nothing.'

In the late afternoon when the water was warmer she bathed
10 with me. She'd spend some time throwing pebbles at a flat stone in the middle of the pool. 'I've seen him. He hasn't died or gone to any other river. He's still there. The land crabs are harmless. People *say* they are harmless. I wouldn't like to –'

'Nor would I. Horrible looking creatures.'

15 She was undecided, uncertain about facts – any fact. When I asked her if the snakes we sometimes saw were poisonous, she said, 'Not those. The *fer de lance* of course, but there are none here,' and added, 'but how can they be sure? Do you think they know?' Then, 'Our snakes are not poisonous. Of course not.'

20 However, she was certain about the monster crab and one afternoon when I was watching her, hardly able to believe she was the pale silent creature I had married, watching her in her blue chemise, blue with white spots, hitched up far above her knees, she stopped laughing, called a warning and threw a large pebble. She threw like
25 a boy, with a sure graceful movement, and I looked down at very long pincer claws, jagged-edged and sharp, vanishing.

'He won't come after you if you keep away from that stone. He lives there. Oh it's another sort of crab. I don't know the name in English. Very big, very old.'

30 As we were walking home I asked her who had taught her to aim so well. 'Oh, Sandi taught me, a boy you never met.'

Every evening we saw the sun go down from the thatched shelter she called the *ajoupa*, I the summer house. We watched the sky and the distant sea on fire – all colours were in that fire and the
35 huge clouds fringed and shot with flame. But I soon tired of the

display. I was waiting for the scent of the flowers by the river – they opened when darkness came and it came quickly. Not night or darkness as I knew it but night with blazing stars, an alien moon – night full of strange noises. Still night, not day.

'The man who owns Consolation Estate is a hermit,' she was   5
saying. 'He never sees anyone – hardly ever speaks, they say.'

'A hermit neighbour suits me. Very well indeed.'

'There are four hermits in this island,' she said. 'Four real ones. Others pretend but they leave when the rainy season comes. Or else they are drunk all the time. That's when sad things happen.'   10

'So this place is as lonely as it feels?' I asked her.

'Yes it is lonely. Are you happy here?'

'Who wouldn't be?'

'I love it more than anywhere in the world. As if it were a person. More than a person.'   15

'But you don't know the world,' I teased her.

'No, only here, and Jamaica of course. Coulibri, Spanish Town. I don't know the other islands at all. Is the world more beautiful, then?'

And how to answer that? 'It's different,' I said.   20

She told me that for a long time they had not known what was happening at Granbois. 'When Mr Mason came' (she always called her stepfather Mr Mason) 'the forest was swallowing it up.' The overseer drank, the house was dilapidated, all the furniture had been stolen, then Baptiste was discovered. A butler. In St Kitts.   25
But born in this island and willing to come back. 'He's a very good overseer,' she'd say, and I'd agree, keeping my opinion of Baptiste, Christophine and all the others to myself. 'Baptiste says . . . Christophine wants . . .'

She trusted them and I did not. But I could hardly say so. Not   30
yet.

We did not see a great deal of them. The kitchen and the swarming kitchen life were some way off. As for the money which she handed out so carelessly, not counting it, not knowing how much she gave, or the unfamiliar faces that appeared then dis-   35
appeared, though never without a large meal eaten and a shot of

rum I discovered – sisters, cousins, aunts and uncles – if she asked no questions how could I?

The house was swept and dusted very early, usually before I woke. Hilda brought coffee and there were always two roses on the
5 tray. Sometimes she'd smile a sweet childish smile, sometimes she would giggle very loudly and rudely, bang the tray down and run away.

'Stupid little girl,' I'd say.

'No, no. She is shy. The girls here are very shy.'

10 After breakfast at noon there'd be silence till the evening meal which was served much later than in England. Christophine's whims and fancies, I was sure. Then we were left alone. Sometimes a sidelong look or a sly knowing glance disturbed me, but it was never for long. 'Not now,' I would think. 'Not yet.'

It was often raining when I woke during the night, a light capricious shower, dancing playful rain, or hushed, muted, growing louder, more persistent, more powerful, an inexorable sound. But always music, a music I had never heard before.

Then I would look at her for long minutes by candlelight, wonder
20 why she seemed sad asleep, and curse the fever or the caution that had made me so blind, so feeble, so hesitating. I'd remember her effort to escape. (*No, I am sorry, I do not wish to marry you.*) Had she given way to that man Richard's arguments, threats probably, I wouldn't trust him far, or to my half-serious blandishments and
25 promises? In any case she had given way, but coldly, unwillingly, trying to protect herself with silence and a blank face. Poor weapons, and they had not served her well or lasted long. If I have forgotten caution, she has forgotten silence and coldness.

Shall I wake her up and listen to the things she says, whispers,
30 in darkness. Not by day.

'I never wished to live before I knew you. I always thought it would be better if I died. Such a long time to wait before it's over.'

'And did you ever tell anyone this?'

'There was no one to tell, no one to listen. Oh you can't imagine
35 Coulibri.'

'But after Coulibri?'

'After Coulibri it was too late. I did not change.'

All day she'd be like any other girl, smile at herself in her looking-glass (*do you like this scent?*), try to teach me her songs, for they haunted me.

Adieu foulard, adieu madras, or *Ma belle ka di maman li*. My beautiful girl said to her mother (*No it is not like that. Now listen. It is this way*). She'd be silent, or angry for no reason, and chatter to Christophine in patois.

'Why do you hug and kiss Christophine?' I'd say.

'Why not?'

'*I* wouldn't hug and kiss them,' I'd say, 'I couldn't.'

At this she'd laugh for a long time and never tell me why she laughed.

But at night how different, even her voice was changed. Always this talk of death. (Is she trying to tell me that is the secret of this place? That there is no other way? She knows. She knows.)

'Why did you make me want to live? Why did you do that to me?'

'Because I wished it. Isn't that enough?'

'Yes, it is enough. But if one day you didn't wish it. What should I do then? Suppose you took this happiness away when I wasn't looking . . .' → *exactly what he does*

'And lose my own? Who'd be so foolish?'

'I am not used to happiness,' she said. 'It makes me afraid.'

'Never be afraid. Or if you are tell no one.'

'I understand. But trying does not help me.'

'What would?' She did not answer that, then one night whispered, 'If I could die. Now, when I am happy. Would you do that? You wouldn't have to kill me. Say die and I will die. You don't believe me? Then try, try, say die and watch me die.'

'Die then! Die!' I watched her die many times. In my way, not in hers. In sunlight, in shadow, by moonlight, by candlelight. In the long afternoons when the house was empty. Only the sun was there to keep us company. We shut him out. And why not? Very soon she was as eager for what's called loving as I was – more lost and drowned afterwards.

passionate moment, height of their 'love'. she is afraid of him taking that away. He has the control.

reference to all the sex they have

She said, 'Here I can do as I like,' not I, and then I said it too. It seemed right in that lonely place. 'Here I can do as I like.'

We seldom met anyone when we left the house. If we did they'd greet us and go on their way.

5 I grew to like these mountain people, silent, reserved, never servile, never curious (or so I thought), not knowing that their quick sideways looks saw everything they wished to see.

It was at night that I felt danger and would try to forget it and push it away.

10 'You are safe,' I'd say. She'd liked that – to be told 'you are safe.' Or I'd touch her face gently and touch tears. Tears – nothing! Words – less than nothing. As for the happiness I gave her, that was worse than nothing. I did not love her. I was thirsty for her, but that is not love. I felt very little tenderness for her,

15 she was a stranger to me, a stranger who did not think or feel as I did.

One afternoon the sight of a dress which she'd left lying on her bedroom floor made me breathless and savage with desire. When I was exhausted I turned away from her and slept, still without a

20 word or a caress. I woke and she was kissing me – soft light kisses. 'It is late,' she said and smiled. 'You must let me cover you up – the land breeze can be cold.'

'And you, aren't you cold?'

'Oh I will be ready quickly. I'll wear the dress you like tonight.'

25 'Yes, do wear it.'

The floor was strewn with garments, hers and mine. She stepped over them carelessly as she walked to her clothes press. 'I was thinking, I'll have another made exactly like it,' she promised happily. 'Will you be pleased?'

30 'Very pleased.'

If she was a child she was not a stupid child but an obstinate one. She often questioned me about England and listened attentively to my answers, but I was certain that nothing I said made much difference. Her mind was already made up. Some romantic novel,

35 a stray remark never forgotten, a sketch, a picture, a song, a waltz, some note of music, and her ideas were fixed. About England and

desire and hatred are reciprocal emotions

about Europe. I could not change them and probably nothing would. Reality might disconcert her, bewilder her, hurt her, but it would not be reality. It would be only a mistake, a misfortune, a wrong path taken, her fixed ideas would never change.

Nothing that I told her influenced her at all.   5

Die then. Sleep. It is all that I can give you . . . wonder if she ever guessed how near she came to dying. In her way, not in mine. It was not a safe game to play – in that place. Desire, Hatred, Life, Death came very close in the darkness. Better not know how close. Better not think, never for a moment. Not close. The same . . .   10
'You are safe,' I'd say to her and to myself. 'Shut your eyes. Rest.'

Then I'd listen to the rain, a sleepy tune that seemed as if it would go on for ever . . . Rain, for ever raining. Drown me in sleep. And soon.   15

Next morning there would be very little sign of these showers. If some of the flowers were battered, the others smelt sweeter, the air was bluer and sparkling fresh. Only the clay path outside my window was muddy. Little shallow pools of water glinted in the hot sun, red earth does not dry quickly.   20

TRAJECTORY BEGINS TO DECLINE

'It came for you this morning early, master,' Amélie said. 'Hilda take it.' She gave me a bulky envelope addressed in careful copperplate. '*By hand. Urgent*' was written in the corner.

'One of our hermit neighbours,' I thought. 'And an enclosure for Antoinette.' Then I saw Baptiste standing near the veranda   25
steps, put the letter in my pocket and forgot it.

I was later than usual that morning but when I was dressed I sat for a long time listening to the waterfall, eyes half closed, drowsy and content. When I put my hand in my pocket for my watch, I touched the envelope and opened it.   30

letter gives Daniel power ; plant seeds of doubt in Rochester's mind

Dear Sir. I take up my pen after long thought and meditation but in the end the truth is better than a lie. I have this to say. You have been shamefully deceived by the Mason family. They tell you perhaps that your

not all aspects of the letter are true, but it contains enough truth for Rochester to pause for thought.

Daniel's "obeah" to Rochester

wife's name is Cosway, the English gentleman Mr Mason being her
stepfather only, but they don't tell you what sort of people were these
Cosways. Wicked and detestable slave-owners since generations – yes
everybody hate them in Jamaica and also in this beautiful island where I
5 hope your stay will be long and pleasant in spite of all, for some not worth
sorrow. Wickedness is not the worst. There is madness in that family. Old
Cosway die raving like his father before him.

You ask what proof I have and why I mix myself up in your affairs. I will
answer you. I am your wife's brother by another lady, half-way house as
10 we say. Her father and mine was a shameless man and of all his illegitimates
I am the most unfortunate and poverty stricken.

My momma die when I was quite small and my godmother take care of
me. The old mister hand out some money for that though he don't like
me. No, that old devil don't like me at all, and when I grow older I see it
15 and I think, Let him wait my day will come. Ask the older people sir about
his disgusting goings on, some will remember.

When Madam his wife die the reprobate marry again quick, to a young
girl from Martinique – it's too much for him. Dead drunk from morning
till night and he die raving and cursing.

20 Then comes the glorious Emancipation Act and trouble for some of the
high and mighties. Nobody would work for the young woman and her two
children and that place Coulibri goes quickly to bush as all does out here
when nobody toil and labour on the land. She have no money and she
have no friends, for French and English like cat and dog in these islands
25 since long time. Shoot, Kill, Everything.

The woman call Christophine also from Martinique stay with her and
an old man Godfrey, too silly to know what happen. Some like that. This
young Mrs Cosway is worthless and spoilt, she can't lift a hand for herself
and soon the madness that is in her, and in all these white Creoles, come
30 out. She shut herself away, laughing and talking to nobody as many can
bear witness. As for the little girl, Antoinetta, as soon as she can walk she
hide herself if she see anybody.

We all wait to hear the woman jump over a precipice '*fini batt's*' as we
say here which mean 'finish to fight'.

35 But no. She marry again to the rich Englishman Mr Mason, and there
is much I could say about that but you won't believe so I shut my mouth.

They say he love her so much that if he have the world on a plate he give it to her – but no use.

The madness gets worse and she has to be shut away for she try to kill her husband – madness not being all either.

That sir is your wife's mother – that was her father. I leave Jamaica. I 5
don't know what happen to the woman. Some say she is dead, other deny it. But old Mason take a great fancy for the girl Antoinetta and give her half his money when he die.

As for me I wander high and low, not much luck but a little money put by and I get to know of a house for sale in this island near Massacre. It's going 10
very cheap so I buy it. News travel even to this wild place and next thing I hear from Jamaica is that old Mason is dead and that family plan to marry the girl to a young Englishman who know nothing of her. Then it seems to me that it is my Christian duty to warn the gentleman that she is no girl to marry with the bad blood she have from both sides. But they are white, I am 15
coloured. They are rich, I am poor. As I think about these things they do it quick while you still weak with fever at the magistrate's, before you can ask questions. If this is true or not you must know for yourself.

Then you come to this island for your honeymoon and it's certain that the Lord put the thing on my shoulders and that it is I must speak the 20
truth to you. Still I hesitate.

I hear you young and handsome with a kind word for all, black, white, also coloured. But I hear too that the girl is beautiful like her mother was beautiful, and you bewitch with her. She is in your blood and your bones. By night and by day. But you, an honourable man, know well that for 25
marriage more is needed than all this. Which does not last. Old Mason bewitch so with her mother and look what happen to him. Sir I pray I am in time to warn you what to do.

Sir ask yourself how I can make up this story and for what reason. When I leave Jamaica I can read write and cypher a little. The good man in 30
Barbados teach me more, he give me books, he tell me read the Bible every day and I pick up knowledge without effort. He is surprise how quick I am. Still I remain an ignorant man and I do not make up this story. I cannot. It is true.

I sit at my window and the words fly past me like birds – with God's 35
help I catch some.

A week this letter take me. I cannot sleep at night thinking what to say. So quickly now I draw to a close and cease my task.

Still you don't believe me? Then ask that devil of a man Richard Mason three questions and make him answer you. Is your wife's mother shut
5 away, a raging lunatic and worse besides? Dead or alive I do not know.

Was your wife's brother an idiot from birth, though God mercifully take him early on?

Is your wife herself going the same way as her mother and all knowing it?

10 Richard Mason is a sly man and he will tell you a lot of nancy stories, which is what we call lies here, about what happen at Coulibri and this and that. Don't listen. Make him answer – yes or no.

If he keep his mouth shut ask others for many think it shameful how that family treat you and your relatives.

15 I beg you sir come to see me for there is more that you should know. But my hand ache, my head ache and my heart is like a stone for the grief I bring you. Money is good but no money can pay for a crazy wife in your bed. Crazy and worse besides.

I lay down my pen with one last request. Come and see me quickly.
20 Your obt servant. Daniel Cosway.

Ask the girl Amélie where I live. She knows, and she knows me. She belongs to this island.

I folded the letter carefully and put it into my pocket. I felt no surprise. It was as if I'd expected it, been waiting for it. For a time,
25 long or short I don't know, I sat listening to the river. At last I stood up, the sun was hot now. I walked stiffly nor could I force myself to think. Then I passed an orchid with long sprays of golden-brown flowers. One of them touched my cheek and I remembered picking some for her one day. 'They are like you,' I
30 told her. Now I stopped, broke a spray off and trampled it into the mud. This brought me to my senses. I leaned against a tree, sweating and trembling. 'Far too hot today,' I said aloud, 'far too hot.' When I came in sight of the house I began to walk silently. No one was about. The kitchen door was shut and the place looked
35 deserted. I went up the steps and along the veranda and when I

heard voices stopped behind the door which led into Antoinette's room. I could see it reflected in the looking-glass. She was in bed and the girl Amélie was sweeping.

'Finish quickly,' said Antoinette, 'and go and tell Christophine I want to see her.' 5

Amélie rested her hands on the broom handle. 'Christophine is going,' she said.

'Going?' repeated Antoinette.

'Yes, going,' said Amélie. 'Christophine don't like this sweet honeymoon house.' Turning round she saw me and laughed loudly. 10 'Your husban' he outside the door and he look like he see zombi. Must be he tired of the sweet honeymoon too.'

Antoinette jumped out of bed and slapped her face.

'I hit you back white cockroach, I hit you back,' said Amélie. And she did. 15

Antoinette gripped her hair. Amélie, whose teeth were bared, seemed to be trying to bite.

'Antoinette, for God's sake,' I said from the doorway.

She swung round, very pale. Amélie buried her face in her hands and pretended to sob, but I could see her watching me through her 20 fingers.

'Go away, child,' I said.

'You call her child,' said Antoinette. 'She is older than the devil himself, and the devil is not more cruel.'

'Send Christophine up,' I said to Amélie. 25

'Yes master, yes master,' she answered softly, dropping her eyes. But as soon as she was out of the room she began to sing:

> 'The white cockroach she marry
> The white cockroach she marry
> The white cockroach she buy young man 30
> The white cockroach she marry.'

Antoinette took a few steps forward. She walked unsteadily. I went to help her but she pushed me away, sat on the bed and with clenched teeth pulled at the sheet, then made a clicking sound of annoyance. She took a pair of scissors from the round table, cut 35 through the hem and tore the sheet in half, then each half into strips.

The noise she made prevented me from hearing Christophine come in, but Antoinette heard her.

5 'You're not leaving?' she said.

'Yes,' said Christophine.

'And what will become of me?' said Antoinette.

'Get up, girl, and dress yourself. Woman must have spunks to live in this wicked world.'

10 She had changed into a drab cotton dress and taken off her heavy gold ear-rings.

'I see enough trouble,' she said. 'I have right to my rest. I have my house that your mother give me so long ago and I have my garden and my son to work for me. A lazy boy but I make him 15 work. Too besides the young master don't like me, and perhaps I don't like him so much. If I stay here I bring trouble and bone of contention in your house.'

'If you are not happy here then go,' said Antoinette.

Amélie came into the room with two jugs of hot water. She 20 looked at me sideways and smiled.

Christophine said in a soft voice, 'Amélie. Smile like that once more, just once more, and I mash your face like I mash plantain. You hear me? Answer me, girl.'

'Yes, Christophine,' Amélie said. She looked frightened.

25 'And too besides I give you bellyache like you never see bellyache. Perhaps you lie a long time with the bellyache I give you. Perhaps you don't get up again with the bellyache I give you. So keep yourself quiet and decent. You hear me?'

'Yes, Christophine,' Amélie said and crept out of the room.

30 'She worthless and good for nothing,' said Christophine with contempt. 'She creep and crawl like centipede.'

She kissed Antoinette on the cheek. Then she looked at me, shook her head, and muttered in patois before she went out.

'Did you hear what that girl was singing?' Antoinette said.

35 'I don't always understand what they say or sing.' Or anything else.

'It was a song about a white cockroach. That's me. That's what
they call all of us who were here before their own people in Africa
sold them to the slave traders. And I've heard English women call us
white niggers. So between you I often wonder who I am and where
is my country and where do I belong and why was I ever born at all.   5
Will you go now please. I must dress like Christophine said.'

After I had waited half an hour I knocked at her door. There was
no answer so I asked Baptiste to bring me something to eat. He
was sitting under the Seville orange tree at the end of the veranda.
He served the food with such a mournful expression that I thought   10
these people are very vulnerable. How old was I when I learned to
hide what I felt? A very small boy. Six, five, even earlier. It was
necessary, I was told, and that view I have always accepted. If these
mountains challenge me, or Baptiste's face, or Antoinette's eyes,
they are mistaken, melodramatic, unreal (England must be quite   15
unreal and like a dream she said).

The rum punch I had drunk was very strong and after the meal
was over I had a great wish to sleep. And why not? This is the time
when everyone sleeps. I imagined the dogs the cats the cocks and
hens all sleeping, even the water in the river running more slowly.   20

I woke up, thought at once of Antoinette and opened the door
into her room, but she was sleeping too. Her back was towards me
and she was quite still. I looked out of the window. The silence
was disturbing, absolute. I would have welcomed the sound of a
dog barking, a man sawing wood. Nothing. Silence. Heat. It was   25
five minutes to three.

I went out following the path I could see from my window. It
must have rained heavily during the night for the red clay was very
muddy. I passed a sparse plantation of coffee trees, then straggly
guava bushes. As I walked I remembered my father's face and his   30
thin lips, my brother's round conceited eyes. They knew. And
Richard the fool, he knew too. And the girl with her blank smiling
face. They all knew.

I began to walk very quickly, then stopped because the light was

different. A green light. I had reached the forest and you cannot mistake the forest. It is hostile. The path was overgrown but it was possible to follow it. I went on without looking at the tall trees on either side. Once I stepped over a fallen log swarming with white
5 ants. How can one discover truth I thought and that thought led me nowhere. No one would tell me the truth. Not my father nor Richard Mason, certainly not the girl I had married. I stood still, so sure I was being watched that I looked over my shoulder. Nothing but the trees and the green light under the trees. A track
10 was just visible and I went on, glancing from side to side and sometimes quickly behind me. This was why I stubbed my foot on a stone and nearly fell. The stone I had tripped on was not a boulder but part of a paved road. There had been a paved road through this forest. The track led to a large clear space. Here were
15 the ruins of a stone house and round the ruins rose trees that had grown to an incredible height. At the back of the ruins a wild orange tree covered with fruit, the leaves a dark green. A beautiful place. And calm – so calm that it seemed foolish to think or plan. What had I to think about and how could I plan? Under the orange
20 tree I noticed little bunches of flowers tied with grass.

I don't know how long it was before I began to feel chilly. The light had changed and the shadows were long. I had better get back before dark, I thought. Then I saw a little girl carrying a large basket on her head. I met her eyes and to my astonishment she
25 screamed loudly, threw up her arms and ran. The basket fell off, I called after her, but she screamed again and ran faster. She sobbed as she ran, a small frightened sound. Then she disappeared. I must be within a few minutes of the path I thought, but after I had walked for what seemed a long time I found that the undergrowth
30 and creepers caught at my legs and the trees closed over my head. I decided to go back to the clearing and start again, with the same result. It was getting dark. It was useless to tell myself that I was not far from the house. I was lost and afraid among these enemy trees, so certain of danger that when I heard footsteps and a shout
35 I did not answer. The footsteps and the voice came nearer. Then I shouted back. I did not recognize Baptiste at first. He was wearing

blue cotton trousers pulled up above his knees and a broad ornamented belt round his slim waist. His machete was in his hand and
the light caught the razor-sharp blue-white edge. He did not smile
when he saw me.

'We look for you a long time,' he said. 5

'I got lost.'

He grunted in answer and led the way, walking in front of me
very quickly and cutting off any branch or creeper that stopped us
with an easy swing of his machete.

I said, 'There was a road here once, where did it lead to?' 10

'No road,' he said.

'But I saw it. A *pavé* road like the French made in the islands.'

'No road.'

'Who lived in that house?'

'They say a priest. Père Lilièvre. He lived here a long time ago.' 15

'A child passed,' I said. 'She seemed very frightened when she
saw me. Is there something wrong about the place?' He shrugged
his shoulders. *he was mistaken for a zombie*

'Is there a ghost, a zombi there?' I persisted.

'Don't know nothing about all that foolishness.' 20

'There was a road here sometime.'

'No road,' he repeated obstinately.

It was nearly dark when we were back on the red clay path. He
walked more slowly, turned and smiled at me. It was as if he'd put
his service mask on the savage reproachful face I had seen. 25

'You don't like the woods at night?'

He did not answer, but pointed to a light and said, 'It's a long
time I've been looking for you. Miss Antoinette frightened you
come to harm.'

When we reached the house I felt very weary. 30

'You like you catch fever,' he said.

'I've had that already.'

'No limit to times you catch fever.'

There was no one on the veranda and no sound from the house.
We both stood in the road looking up, then he said, 'I send the girl 35
to you, master.'

65

Hilda brought me a large bowl of soup and some fruit. I tried the door into Antoinette's room. It was bolted and there was no light. Hilda giggled. A nervous giggle.

I told her that I did not want anything to eat, to bring me the
5 decanter of rum and a glass. I drank, then took up the book I had been reading, *The Glittering Coronet of Isles* it was called, and I turned to the chapter 'Obeah':

Rhys plays with this definition ·

'A zombi is a dead person who seems to be alive or a living person who is dead. A zombi can also be the spirit of a place, usually malignant but
10 sometimes to be propitiated with sacrifices or offerings of flowers and fruit.' [I thought at once of the bunches of flowers at the priest's ruined house.] ' "They cry out in the wind that is their voice, they rage in the sea that is their anger." '

'So I was told, but I have noticed that negroes as a rule refuse to discuss
15 the black magic in which so many believe. Voodoo as it is called in Haiti – Obeah in some of the islands, another name in South America. They confuse matters by telling lies if pressed. The white people, sometimes credulous, pretend to dismiss the whole thing as nonsense. Cases of sudden or mysterious death are attributed to a poison known to the negroes which
20 cannot be traced. It is further complicated by . . .'

Antoinette going up to Christophene → tradjectory up again

I did not look up though I saw him at the window but rode on without thinking till I came to the rocks. People here call them Mounes Mors (the Dead Ones). Preston shied at them, they say horses always do. Then he stumbled badly, so I dismounted and
25 walked along with the bridle over my arm. It was getting hot and I was tired when I reached the path to Christophine's two-roomed house, the roof shingled, not thatched. She was sitting on a box under her mango tree, smoking a white clay pipe and she called out, 'It's you, Antoinette? Why you come up here so early?'
30 'I just wanted to see you,' I said.

She helped me loosen Preston's girth and led him to a stream near by. He drank as if he were very thirsty, then shook himself and snorted. Water flew out of his nostrils. We left him cropping grass and went back to the mango tree. She sat on her box and pushed another towards me, but I knelt close to her touching a thin silver bangle that she always wore.

'You smell the same,' I said.

'You come all this long way to tell me that?' she said. Her clothes smelled of clean cotton, starched and ironed. I had seen her so often standing knee deep in the river at Coulibri, her long skirt hitched up, washing her dresses and her white shifts, then beating them against the stones. Sometimes there would be other women all bringing their washing down on the stones again and again, a gay busy noise. At last they would spread the wet clothes in the sun, wipe their foreheads, start laughing and talking. She smelled too, of their smell, so warm and comforting to me (but he does not like it). The sky was dark blue through the dark green mango leaves, and I thought, 'This is my place and this is where I belong and this is where I wish to stay.' Then I thought, 'What a beautiful tree, but it is too high up here for mangoes and it may never bear fruit,' and I thought of lying alone in my bed with the soft silk cotton mattress and fine sheets, listening. At last I said, 'Christophine, he does not love me, I think he hates me. He always sleeps in his dressing-room now and the servants know. If I get angry he is scornful and silent, sometimes he does not speak to me for hours and I cannot endure it any more, I cannot. What shall I do? He was not like that at first,' I said.

Pink and red hibiscus grew in front of her door, she lit her pipe and did not answer.

'Answer me,' I said. She puffed out a cloud of smoke.

'You ask me a hard thing, I tell you a hard thing, pack up and go.'

'Go, go where? To some strange place where I shall never see him? No, I will not, then everyone, not only the servants, will laugh at me.'

'It's not you they laugh at if you go, they laugh at him.'

'I will not do that.'

'Why you ask me, if when I answer you say no? Why you come up here if when I tell you the truth, you say no?'

'But there must be something else I can do.'

She looked gloomy. 'When man don't love you, more you try, more he hate you, man like that. If you love them they treat you bad, if you don't love them they after you night and day bothering
5 your soul case out. I hear about you and your husband,' she said.

'But I cannot go. He is my husband after all.'

She spat over her shoulder. 'All women, all colours, nothing but fools. Three children I have. One living in this world, each one a different father, but no husband, I thank my God. I keep my
10 money. I don't give it to no worthless man.'

'When must I go, where must I go?'

'But look me trouble, a rich white girl like you and more foolish than the rest. A man don't treat you good, pick up your skirt and walk out. Do it and he come after you.'

15 'He will not come after me. And you must understand I am not rich now, I have no money of my own at all, everything I had belongs to him.'

'What you tell me there?' she said sharply.

'That is English law.'

20 'Law! The Mason boy fix it, that boy worse than Satan and he burn in Hell one of these fine nights. Listen to me now and I advise you what to do. Tell your husband you feeling sick, you want to visit your cousin in Martinique. Ask him pretty for some of your own money, the man not bad-hearted, he give it. When you get
25 away, stay away. Ask more. He give again and well satisfy. In the end he come to find out what you do, how you get on without him, and if he see you fat and happy he want you back. Men like that. Better not stay in that old house. Go from that house, I tell you.'

'You think I must leave him?'

30 'You ask me so I answer.'

'Yes,' I said. 'After all I could, but why should I go to Martinique? I wish to see England, I might be able to borrow money for that. Not from him but I know how I might get it. I must travel far, if I go.'

35 I have been too unhappy, I thought, it cannot last, being so unhappy, it would kill you. I will be a different person when I live

in England and different things will happen to me. . . . England, rosy pink in the geography book map, but on the page opposite the words are closely crowded, heavy looking. Exports, coal, iron, wool. Then Imports and Character of Inhabitants. Names, Essex, Chelmsford on the Chelmer. The Yorkshire and Lincolnshire wolds. Wolds? Does that mean hills? How high? Half the height of ours, or not even that? Cool green leaves in the short cool summer. Summer. There are fields of corn like sugar-cane fields, but gold colour and not so tall. After summer the trees are bare, then winter and snow. White feathers falling? Torn pieces of paper falling? They say frost makes flower patterns on the window panes. I must know more than I know already. For I know that house where I will be cold and not belonging, the bed I shall lie in has red curtains and I have slept there many times before, long ago. How long ago? In that bed I will dream the end of my dream. But my dream had nothing to do with England and I must not think like this, I must remember about chandeliers and dancing, about swans and roses and snow. And snow.

'England,' said Christophine, who was watching me. 'You think there is such a place?'

'How can you ask that? You know there is.'

'I never see the damn place, how I know?'

'You do not believe that there is a country called England?'

She blinked and answered quickly, 'I don't say I don't *believe*, I say I don't *know*, I know what I see with my eyes and I never see it. Besides I ask myself is this place like they tell us? Some say one thing, some different, I hear it cold to freeze your bones and they thief your money, clever like the devil. You have money in your pocket, you look again and bam! No money. Why you want to go to this cold thief place? If there is this place at all, I never see it, that is one thing sure.'

I stared at her, thinking, 'but how can she know the best thing for me to do, this ignorant, obstinate old negro woman, who is not certain if there is such a place as England?' She knocked out her pipe and stared back at me, her eyes had no expression at all.

'Christophine,' I said, 'I may do as you advise. But not yet.'

(Now, I thought, I must say what I came to say.) 'You knew what I wanted as soon as you saw me, and you certainly know now. Well, don't you?' I heard my voice getting high and thin.

'Hush up,' she said. 'If the man don't love you, I can't make him
5 love you.'

'Yes you can, I know you can. That is what I wish and that is why I came here. You can make people love or hate. Or . . . or die,' I said.

She threw back her head and laughed loudly. (But she never
10 laughs loudly and why is she laughing at all?)

'So you believe in that tim-tim story about obeah, you hear when you so high? All that foolishness and folly. Too besides, that is not for *béké*. Bad, bad trouble come when *béké* meddle with that.'

'You must,' I said. 'You must.'

15 'Hush up. Jo-jo my son coming to see me, if he catch you crying, he tell everybody.'

'I will be quiet, I will not cry. But Christophine, if he, my husband, could come to me one night. Once more. I would make him love me.'

20 'No *doudou*. No.'

'Yes, Christophine.'

'You talk foolishness. Even if I can make him come to your bed, I cannot make him love you. Afterward he hate you.'

'No. And what do I care if he does? He hates me now. I hear
25 him every night walking up and down the veranda. Up and down. When he passes my door he says, "Goodnight, Bertha." He never calls me Antoinette now. He has found out it was my mother's name. "I hope you will sleep well, Bertha" – it cannot be worse,' I said. 'That one night he came I might sleep afterwards. I sleep so
30 badly now. And I dream.'

'No, I don't meddle with that for you.'

Then I beat my fist on a stone, forcing myself to speak calmly.

'Going away to Martinique or England or anywhere else, that is the lie. He would never give me any money to go away and he
35 would be furious if I asked him. There would be a scandal if I left him and he hates scandal. Even if I got away (and how?) he

would force me back. So would Richard. So would everybody else. Running away from him, from this island, is the lie. What reason could I give for going and who would believe me?'

When she bent her head she looked old and I thought, 'Oh Christophine, do not grow old. You are the only friend I have, do 5 not go away from me into being old.'

'Your husband certainly love money,' she said. 'That is no lie. Money have pretty face for everybody, but for that man money pretty like pretty self, he can't see nothing else.'

'Help me then.' 10

'Listen *doudou ché*. Plenty people fasten bad words on you and on your mother. I know it. I know who is talking and what they say. The man not a bad man, even if he love money, but he hear so many stories he don't know what to believe. That is why he keep away. I put no trust in none of those people round you. Not here, 15 not in Jamaica.'

'Not Aunt Cora?'

'Your aunty old woman now, she turn her face to the wall.'

'*How do you know?*' I said. For that is what happened.

When I passed her room, I heard her quarrelling with Richard 20 and I knew it was about my marriage. 'It's disgraceful,' she said. 'It's shameful. You are handing over everything the child owns to a perfect stranger. Your father would never have allowed it. She should be protected, legally. A settlement can be arranged and it should be arranged. That was his intention.' 25

'You are talking about an honourable gentleman, not a rascal,' Richard said. 'I am not in a position to make conditions, as you know very well. She is damn lucky to get him, all things considered. Why should I insist on a lawyer's settlement when I trust him? I would trust him with my life,' he went on in an affected voice. 30

'You are trusting him with her life, not yours,' she said.

He told her for God's sake shut up you old fool and banged the door when he left. So angry that he did not notice me standing in the passage. She was sitting up in bed when I went into her room. 'Halfwit that the boy is, or pretends to be. I do not like what I have 35 seen of this honourable gentleman. Stiff. Hard as a board and

71

stupid as a foot, in my opinion, except where his own interests are concerned.'

She was very pale and shaking all over, so I gave her the smelling salts on the dressing-table. They were in a red glass bottle with a gilt
5 top. She put the bottle to her nose but her hand dropped as though she were too tired to hold it steady. Then she turned away from the window, the sky, the looking-glass, the pretty things on the dressing-table. The red and gilt bottle fell to the floor. She turned her face to the wall. 'The Lord has forsaken us,' she said, and shut her eyes. She
10 did not speak again, and after a while I thought she was asleep. She was too ill to come to my wedding and I went to say good-bye, I was excited and happy thinking now it is my honeymoon. I kissed her and she gave me a little silk bag. 'My rings. Two are valuable. Don't show it to him. Hide it away. Promise me.'

15 I promised, but when I opened it, one of the rings was plain gold. I thought I might sell another yesterday but who will buy what I have to sell here? . . . ⸢ playing the role of mother, trying to instill courage in Antoinette.

Christophine was saying, 'Your aunty too old and sick, and that Mason boy worthless. Have spunks and do battle for yourself.
20 Speak to your husband calm and cool, tell him about your mother and all what happened at Coulibri and why she get sick and what they do to her. Don't bawl at the man and don't make crazy faces. Don't cry either. Crying no good with him. Speak nice and make him understand.' → giving her motherly advice

25 'I have tried,' I said, 'but he does not believe me. It is too late for that now' (it is always too late for truth, I thought). 'I will try again if you will do what I ask. Oh Christophine, I am so afraid,' I said, 'I do not know why, but so afraid. All the time. Help me.'

She said something I did not hear. Then she took a sharp stick
30 and drew lines and circles on the earth under the tree, then rubbed them out with her foot.

'If you talk to him first I do what you ask me.'

'Now?'

'Yes,' she said. 'Now look at me. Look in my eyes.'

35 I was giddy when I stood up, and she went into the house muttering and came out with a cup of coffee.

'Good shot of white rum in that,' she said. 'Your face like dead woman and your eyes red like *soucriant*. Keep yourself quiet – look, Jo-jo coming, he talk to everybody about what he hear. Nothing but leaky calabash that boy.'

When I had drunk the coffee I began to laugh. 'I have been so unhappy for nothing, nothing,' I said.

Her son was carrying a large basket on his head. I watched his strong brown legs swinging along the path so easily. He seemed surprised and inquisitive when he saw me, but he asked politely in patois, was I well, was the master in good health?

'Yes, Jo-jo, thank you, we are both well.'

Christophine helped him with the basket, then she brought out the bottle of white rum and poured out half a tumblerful. He swallowed it quickly. Then she filled the glass with water and he drank that like they do.

She said in English, 'The mistress is going, her horse at the back there. Saddle him up.'

I followed her into the house. There was a wooden table in the outer room, a bench and two broken-down chairs. Her bedroom was large and dark. She still had her bright patchwork counterpane, the palm leaf from Palm Sunday and the prayer for a happy death. But after I noticed a heap of chicken feathers in one corner, I did not look round any more.

'So already you frightened ch?' And when I saw her expression I took my purse from my pocket and threw it on the bed.

'You don't have to give me money. I do this foolishness because you beg me – not for money.'

'Is it foolishness?' I said, whispering and she laughed again, but softly.

'If *béké* say it foolishness, then it foolishness. *Béké* clever like the devil. More clever than God. Ain't so? Now listen and I will tell you what to do.'

When we came out into the sunlight, Jo-jo was holding Preston near a big stone. I stood on it and mounted.

'Good-bye, Christophine; good-bye, Jo-jo.'

'Good-bye, mistress.'

where does the betrayal lie?
Both Christophene and Rochester
are forced to do things they don't
want to.

'You will come and see me very soon, Christophine?'

'Yes, I will come.'

I looked back at the end of the path. She was talking to Jo-jo and he seemed curious and amused. Nearby a cock crowed and I
5 thought, 'That is for betrayal, but who is the traitor?' She did not want to do this. I forced her with my ugly money. And what does anyone know about traitors, or why Judas did what he did?

I can remember every second of that morning, if I shut my eyes I can see the deep blue colour of the sky and the mango leaves, the
10 pink and red hibiscus, the yellow handkerchief she wore round her head, tied in the Martinique fashion with the sharp points in front, but now I see everything still, fixed for ever like the colours in a stained-glass window. Only the clouds move. It was wrapped in a leaf, what she had given me, and I felt it cool and smooth against
15 my skin.

indefinite again

First indication of her losing sanity, and losing her identity.
Dying, become a zombie ★

'The mistress pay a visit,' Baptiste told me when he brought my coffee that morning. 'She will come back tonight or tomorrow. She make up her mind in a hurry and she has gone.'

shift in
narration
AGAIN
>unclear

In the afternoon Amélie brought me a second letter.

20 Why you don't answer. You don't believe me? Then ask someone else – everybody in Spanish Town know. Why you think they bring you to this place? You want me to come to your house and bawl out your business before everybody? You come to me or I come –

effective
technique
because
the reader
loses touch
with reality
like the
characters
do.

At this point I stopped reading. The child Hilda came into the
25 room and I asked her, 'Is Amélie here?'

'Yes, master.'

'Tell her I wish to speak to her.'

'Yes, master.'

She put her hand over her mouth as if to stifle laughter, but her
30 eyes, which were the blackest I had ever seen, so black that it was impossible to distinguish the pupil from the iris, were alarmed and bewildered.

I sat on the veranda with my back to the sea and it was as if I

74

had done it all my life. I could not imagine different weather or a
different sky. I knew the shape of the mountains as well as I knew
the shape of the two brown jugs filled with white sweet-scented
flowers on the wooden table. I knew that the girl would be wearing
a white dress. Brown and white she would be, her curls, her white   5
girl's hair she called it, half covered with a red handkerchief, her
feet bare. There would be the sky and the mountains, the flowers
and the girl and the feeling that all this was a nightmare, the faint
consoling hope that I might wake up.

She leaned lightly against the veranda post, indifferently graceful, 10
just respectful enough, and waited.

'Was this letter given to you?' I asked.

'No, master. Hilda take it.'

'And is this man who writes a friend of yours?'

'Not my friend,' she said.   15

'But he knows you – or says he does.'

'Oh yes, I know Daniel.'

'Very well then. Will you tell him that his letters annoy me, and
that he'd better not write again for his own sake. If he brings a
letter give it back to him. Understand?'   20

'Yes, master. I understand.'

Still leaning against the post she smiled at me, and I felt that at
any moment her smile would become loud laughter. It was to stop
this that I went on, 'Why does he write to me?'

She answered innocently, 'He don't tell you that? He write you   25
two letters and he don't say why he is writing? If you don't know
then I don't know.'

'But you know him?' I said. 'Is his name Cosway?'

'Some people say yes, some people say no. That's what he calls
himself.'   30

She added thoughtfully that Daniel was a very superior man,
always reading the Bible and that he lived like white people. I tried
to find out what she meant by this, and she explained that he had
a house like white people, with one room only for sitting. That he
had two pictures on the wall of his father and his mother.   35

'White people?'

'Oh no, coloured.'

'But he told me in his first letter that his father was a white man.'

She shrugged her shoulders. 'All that too long ago for me.' It was easy to see her contempt for long ago. 'I tell him what you say, master.' Then she added, 'Why you don't go and see him? It is much better. Daniel is a bad man and he will come here and make trouble for you. It's better he don't come. They say one time he was a preacher in Barbados, he talk like a preacher, and he have a brother in Jamaica in Spanish Town, Mr Alexander. Very wealthy man. He own three rum shops and two dry goods stores.' She flicked a look at me as sharp as a knife. 'I hear one time that Miss Antoinette and his son Mr Sandi get married, but that all foolishness. Miss Antoinette a white girl with a lot of money, she won't marry with a coloured man even though he don't look like a coloured man. You ask Miss Antoinette, she tell you.'

Like Hilda she put her hand over her mouth as though she could not stop herself from laughing and walked away.

Then turned and said in a very low voice, 'I am sorry for you.'

'What did you say?'

'I don't say nothing, master.'

Antoinette seeking Christophene's help
// Rochester seeking Daniel.
But Rochester goes DOWN to see him.

A large table covered with a red fringed cloth made the small room seem hotter; the only window was shut.

'I put your chair near the door,' Daniel said, 'a breeze come in from underneath.' But there was no breeze, not a breath of air, this place was lower down the mountain almost at sea-level.

'When I hear you coming I take a good shot of rum, and then I take a glass of water to cool me down, but it don't cool me down, it run out of my eyes in tears and lamentations. Why don't you give me an answer when I write to you the first time?' He went on talking, his eyes fixed on a framed text hanging on the dirty white wall, 'Vengeance is Mine'.

'You take too long, Lord,' he told it. 'I hurry you up a bit.' Then he wiped his thin yellow face and blew his nose on a corner of the tablecloth.

biblical allusion - Brother of Jacob,
eldest son sold his birthright for a
pot of stew.

Part Two

'They call me Daniel,' he said, still not looking at me, 'but my
name is Esau. All I get is curses and get-outs from that damn devil
my father. My father old Cosway, with his white marble tablet in the
English church at Spanish Town for all to see. It have a crest on it
and a motto in Latin and words in big black letters. I never know   5
such lies. I hope that stone tie round his neck and drag him down to
Hell in the end. "Pious", they write up. "Beloved by all". Not a
word about the people he buy and sell like cattle. "Merciful to the
weak", they write up. Mercy! The man have a heart like stone. Sometimes when he get sick of a woman which is quickly, he free her like   10
he free my mother, even he give her a hut and a bit of land for
herself (a garden some call that), but it is no mercy, it's for wicked
pride he do it. I never put my eyes on a man haughty and proud
like that – he walk like he own the earth. "I don't give a damn," he
says. Let him wait. . . . I can still see that tablet before my eyes   15
because I go to look at it often. I know by heart all the lies they tell –
no one to stand up and say, Why you write lies in the church? . . . I
tell you this so you can know what sort of people you mix up with.
The heart know its own bitterness but to keep it lock up all the time,
that is hard. I remember it like yesterday the morning he put a curse   20
on me. Sixteen years old I was and anxious. I start very early. I walk
all the way to Coulibri – five six hours it take. He don't refuse to see
me; he receive me very cool and calm and first thing he tell me is
I'm always pestering him for money. This because sometimes I ask
help to buy a pair of shoes and such. Not to go barefoot like a   25
nigger. Which I am not. He look at me like I was dirt and I get
angry too. "I have my rights after all," I tell him and you know
what he do? He laugh in my face. When he finished laughing he
call me what's-your-name. "I can't remember all their names – it's
too much to expect of me," he says, talking to himself. Very old he   30
look in the bright sunshine that morning. "It's you yourself call me
Daniel," I tell him. "I'm no slave like my mother was."

' "Your mother was a sly-boots if ever there was one," he says,
"and I'm not a fool. However the woman's dead and that's enough.
But if there's one drop of my blood in your spindly carcass I'll eat   35
my hat." By this time my own blood at boiling point, I tell you, so

77

I bawl back at him, "Eat it then. Eat it. You haven't much time.
Not much time either to kiss and love your new wife. She too
young for you." "Great God!" he said and his face go red and then
a kind of grey colour. He try to get up but he falls back in his chair.
5 He have a big silver inkstand on his desk, he throw it at my head
and he curse me, but I duck and the inkstand hit the door. I have
to laugh but I go off quick. He send me some money – not a word,
only the money. It's the last time I see him.'

Daniel breathed deeply and wiped his face again and offered me
10 some rum. When I thanked him and shook my head he poured
himself half a glassful and swallowed it.

'All that long time ago,' he said.

'Why did you wish to see me, Daniel?'

The last drink seemed to have sobered him. He looked at me
15 directly and spoke more naturally.

'I insist because I have this to say. When you ask if what I tell
you is true, you will ask though you don't like me, I see that; but
you know well my letter was no lie. Take care who you talk to.
Many people like to say things behind your back, to your face they
20 get frightened, or they don't want to mix up. The magistrate now,
he know a lot, but his wife very friendly with the Mason family and
she stop him if she can. Then there is my half brother Alexander,
coloured like me but not unlucky like me, he will want to tell you
all sorts of lies. He was the old man's favourite and he prosper right
25 from the start. Yes, Alexander is a rich man now but he keep quiet
about it. Because he prosper he is two-faced, he won't speak against
white people. There is that woman up at your house, Christophine.
She is the worst. She have to leave Jamaica because she go to jail:
you know that?'

30 'Why was she sent to jail? What did she do?'

His eyes slid away from mine. 'I tell you I leave Spanish Town,
I don't know all that happen. It's something very bad. She is obeah
woman and they catch her. I don't believe in all that devil business
but many believe. Christophine is a bad woman and she will lie to
35 you worse than your wife. Your own wife she talks sweet talk and
she lies.'

The black and gilt clock on a shelf struck four.

I must go. I must get away from his yellow sweating face and his hateful little room. I sat still, numb, staring at him.

'You like my clock?' said Daniel. 'I work hard to buy it. But it's to please myself. I don't have to please no woman. Buy me this 5 and buy me that – demons incarnate in my opinion. Alexander now, he can't keep away from them, and in the end he marry a very fair-coloured girl, very respectable family. His son Sandi is like a white man, but more handsome than any white man, and received by many white people they say. Your wife know Sandi 10 since long time. Ask her and she tell you. But not everything I think.' He laughed. 'Oh no, not everything. I see them when they think nobody see them. I see her when she . . . You going eh?' He darted to the doorway.

'No you don't go before I tell you the last thing. You want me 15 to shut my mouth about what I know. She start with Sandi. They fool you well about that girl. She look you straight in the eye and talk sweet talk – and it's lies she tell you. Lies. Her mother was so. They say she worse than her mother, and she hardly more than a child. Must be you deaf you don't hear people laughing when you 20 marry her. Don't waste your anger on me, sir. It's not I fool you, it's I wish to open your eyes. . . . A tall fine English gentleman like you, you don't want to touch a little yellow rat like me eh? Besides I understand well. You believe me, but you want to do everything quiet like the English can. All right. But if I keep my mouth shut it 25 seems to me you owe me something. What is five hundred pounds to you? To me it's my life.'

Now disgust was rising in me like sickness. Disgust and rage.

'All right,' he yelled, and moved away from the door. 'Go then . . . get out. Now it's me to say it. Get out. Get out. And if I don't 30 have the money I want you will see what I can do.

'Give my love to your wife – my sister,' he called after me venomously. 'You are not the first to kiss her pretty face. Pretty face, soft skin, pretty colour – not yellow like me. But my sister just the same . . .' 35

At the end of the path out of sight and sound of the house I *symbolizes lechery, filth.*

stopped. The world was given up to heat and to flies, the light was dazzling after his little dark room. A black and white goat tethered near by was staring at me and for what seemed minutes I stared back into its slanting yellow-green eyes. Then I walked to the tree
5 where I'd left my horse and rode away as quickly as I could.

Rochester leaves poisoned because Daniel implies that Antoinette has slept around → affair w Sandi

The telescope was pushed to one side of the table making room for a decanter half full of rum and two glasses on a tarnished silver tray. I listened to the ceaseless night noises outside, and watched the procession of small moths and beetles fly into the candle flames,
10 then poured out a drink of rum and swallowed. At once the night noises drew away, became distant, bearable, even pleasant.

Antoinette attempts to talk to Rochester.

'Will you listen to me for God's sake,' Antoinette said. She had said this before and I had not answered, now I told her, 'Of course. I'd be the brute you doubtless think me if I did not do that.'
15 'Why do you hate me?' she said.

'I do not hate you, I am most distressed about you, I am distraught,' I said. But this was untrue, I was not distraught, I was calm, it was the first time I had felt calm or self-possessed for many a long day. *→ because he's already made up his mind.*

20 She was wearing the white dress I had admired, but it had slipped untidily over one shoulder and seemed too large for her. I watched her holding her left wrist with her right hand, an annoying habit.

'Then why do you never come near me?' she said. 'Or kiss me, or talk to me. Why do you think I can bear it, what reason have
25 you for treating me like that? Have you any reason?'

'Yes,' I said, 'I have a reason,' and added very softly, 'My God.'

'You are always calling on God,' she said. 'Do you believe in God?'

'Of course, of course I believe in the power and wisdom of my
30 creator.'

She raised her eyebrows and the corners of her mouth turned down in a questioning mocking way. For a moment she looked very much like Amélie. Perhaps they are related, I thought. It's possible, it's even probable in this damned place.

35 'And you,' I said. 'Do you believe in God?'

'It doesn't matter,' she answered calmly, 'what I believe or you believe, because we can do nothing about it, we are like these.' She flicked a dead moth off the table. 'But I asked you a question, you remember. Will you answer that?'

I drank again and my brain was cold and clear.   5

'Very well, but question for question. Is your mother alive?'

'No, she is dead, she died.'

'When?'

'Not long ago.'

'Then why did you tell me that she died when you were a child?'   10

'Because they told me to say so and because it is true. She did die when I was a child. There are always two deaths, the real one and the one people know about.' *killing the spirit/soul, then death of the body*

'Two at least,' I said, 'for the fortunate.' We were silent for a moment, then I went on, 'I had a letter from a man who calls   15 himself Daniel Cosway.'   *no certainty about him*

'He has no right to that name,' she said quickly. 'His real name, if he has one, is Daniel Boyd. He hates all white people, but he hates me the most. He tells lies about us and he is sure that you will believe him and not listen to the other side.'   20

'Is there another side?' I said.   *Why Rhys is writing the book, she is giving us "the other side".*

'There is always the other side, always.'

'After his second letter, which was threatening, I thought it best to go and see him.'

'You saw him,' she said. 'I know what he told you. That my   25 mother was mad and an infamous woman and that my little brother who died was born a cretin, an idiot, and that I am a mad girl too. That is what he told you, isn't it?'

'Yes, that was his story, and is any of it true?' I said, cold and calm.   30

One of the candles flared up and I saw the hollows under her eyes, her drooping mouth, her thin, strained face.

'We won't talk about it now,' I said. 'Rest tonight.'

'But we must talk about it.' Her voice was high and shrill.

'Only if you promise to be reasonable.'   35

But this is not the place or the time, I thought, not in this long dark veranda with the candles burning low and the watching, listening night outside. 'Not tonight,' I said again. 'Some other time.'

'I might never be able to tell you in any other place or at any
5 other time. No other time, now. You frightened?' she said, imitating a Negro's voice, singing and insolent.

Then I saw her shiver and remembered that she had been wearing a yellow silk shawl. I got up (my brain so clear and cold, my body so weighted and heavy). The shawl was on a chair in the next room,
10 there were candles on the sideboard and I brought them on to the veranda, lit two, and put the shawl around her shoulders. 'But why not tell me tomorrow, in the daylight?'

'You have no right,' she said fiercely. 'You have no right to ask questions about my mother and then refuse to listen to my answer.'
15 'Of course I will listen, of course we can talk now, if that's what you wish.' But the feeling of something unknown and hostile was very strong. 'I feel very much a stranger here,' I said. 'I feel that this place is my enemy and on your side.'

'You are quite mistaken,' she said. 'It is not for you and not for
20 me. It has nothing to do with either of us. That is why you are afraid of it, because it is something else. I found that out long ago when I was a child. I loved it because I had nothing else to love, but it is as indifferent as this God you call on so often.'

'We can talk here or anywhere else,' I said, 'just as you wish.'
25 The decanter of rum was nearly empty so I went back into the dining-room, and brought out another bottle of rum. She had eaten nothing and refused wine, now she poured herself a drink, touched it with her lips then put it down again.

'You want to know about my mother, I will tell you about her,
30 the truth, not lies.' Then she was silent for so long that I said gently, 'I know that after your father died, she was very lonely and unhappy.'

'And very poor,' she said. 'Don't forget that. For five years. Isn't it quick to say. And isn't it long to live. And lonely. She was so
35 lonely that she grew away from other people. That happens. It happened to me too but it was easier for me because I hardly

remembered anything else. For her it was strange and frightening. And then she was so lovely. I used to think that every time she looked in the glass she must have hoped and pretended. I pretended too. Different things of course. You can pretend for a long time, but one day it all falls away and you are alone. We were alone in the most beautiful place in the world, it is not possible that there can be anywhere else so beautiful as Coulibri. The sea was not far off but we never heard it, we always heard the river. No sea. It was an old-time house and once there was an avenue of royal palms but a lot of them had fallen and others had been cut down and the ones that were left looked lost. Lost trees. Then they poisoned her horse and she could not ride about any more. She worked in the garden even when the sun was very hot and they'd say "You go in now, mistress."'

'And who were they?'

'Christophine was with us, and Godfrey the old gardener stayed, and a boy, I forget his name. Oh yes,' she laughed. 'His name was Disastrous because his godmother thought it such a pretty word. The parson said, "I cannot christen this child Disastrous, he must have another name," so his name was Disastrous Thomas, we called him Sass. It was Christophine who bought our food from the village and persuaded some girls to help her sweep and wash clothes. We would have died, my mother always said, if she had not stayed with us. Many died in those days, both white and black, especially the older people, but no one speaks of those days now. They are forgotten, except the lies. Lies are never forgotten, they go on and they grow.'

'And you,' I said. 'What about you?'

'I was never sad in the morning,' she said, 'and every day was a fresh day for me. I remember the taste of milk and bread and the sound of the grandfather clock ticking slowly and the first time I had my hair tied with string because there was no ribbon left and no money to buy any. All the flowers in the world were in our garden and sometimes when I was thirsty I licked raindrops from the jasmine leaves after a shower. If I could make you see it, because they destroyed it and it is only here now.' She struck her forehead. 'One of the best things was a curved flight of shallow steps that went down from the *glacis* to the mounting stone, the handrail was ornamented iron.'

'Wrought iron,' I said.

5 'Yes, wrought iron, and at the end of the last step it was curved like a question mark and when I put my hand on it, the iron was warm and I was comforted.'

'But you said you were always happy.'

'No, I said I was always happy in the morning, not always in the
10 afternoon and never after sunset, for after sunset the house was haunted, some places are. Then there was that day when she saw I was growing up like a white nigger and she was ashamed of me, it was after that day that everything changed. Yes, it was my fault, it was my fault that she started to plan and work in a frenzy, in a
15 fever to change our lives. Then people came to see us again and though I still hated them and was afraid of their cool, teasing eyes, I learned to hide it.'

'No,' I said.

'Why no?'

20 'You have never learned to hide it,' I said.

'I learned to try,' said Antoinette. Not very well, I thought.

'And there was that night when they destroyed it.' She lay back in the chair, very pale. I poured some rum out and offered it to her, but she pushed the glass away so roughly that it spilled over her
25 dress. 'There is nothing left now. They trampled on it. It was a sacred place. It was sacred to the sun!' I began to wonder how much of all this was true, how much imagined, distorted. Certainly many of the old estate houses were burned. You saw ruins all over the place.

30 As if she'd guessed my thoughts she went on calmly, 'But I was telling you about my mother. Afterwards I had fever. I was at Aunt Cora's house in Spanish Town. I heard screams and then someone laughing very loud. Next morning Aunt Cora told me that my mother was ill and had gone to the country. This did not seem
35 strange to me for she was part of Coulibri, and if Coulibri had been destroyed and gone out of my life, it seemed natural that she should

go too. I was ill for a long time. My head was bandaged because someone had thrown a stone at me. Aunt Cora told me that it was healing up and that it wouldn't spoil me on my wedding day. But I think it did spoil me for my wedding day and all the other days and nights.' 5

I said, 'Antoinette, your nights are not spoiled, or your days, put the sad things away. Don't think about them and nothing will be spoiled, I promise you.'

But my heart was heavy as lead.

'Pierre died,' she went on as if she had not heard me, 'and my 10 mother hated Mr Mason. She would not let him go near her or touch her. She said she would kill him, she tried to, I think. So he bought her a house and hired a coloured man and woman to look after her. For a while he was sad but he often left Jamaica and spent a lot of time in Trinidad. He almost forgot her.' 15

'And you forgot her too,' I could not help saying.

'I am not a forgetting person,' said Antoinette. 'But she – she didn't want me. She pushed me away and cried when I went to see her. They told me I made her worse. People talked about her, they would not leave her alone, they would be talking about her and 20 stop if they saw me. One day I made up my mind to go to her, by myself. Before I reached her house I heard her crying. I thought I will kill anyone who is hurting my mother. I dismounted and ran quickly on to the veranda where I could look into the room. I remember the dress she was wearing – an evening dress cut very 25 low, and she was barefooted. There was a fat black man with a glass of rum in his hand. He said, "Drink it and you will forget." She drank it without stopping. He poured her some more and she took the glass and laughed and threw it over her shoulder. It smashed to pieces. "Clean it up," the man said to the woman, "or 30 she'll walk in it."

' "If she walk in it a damn good thing," the woman said. "Perhaps she keep quiet then." However she brought a pan and brush and swept up the broken glass. All this I saw. My mother did not look at them. She walked up and down and said, "But this is a very 35 pleasant surprise, Mr Luttrell. Godfrey, take Mr Luttrell's horse."

Then she seemed to grow tired and sat down in the rocking-chair.
I saw the man lift her up out of the chair and kiss her. I saw his
mouth fasten on hers and she went all soft and limp in his arms
and he laughed. The woman laughed too, but she was angry. When
5 I saw that I ran away. Christophine was waiting for me when I
came back crying. "What you want to go up there for?" she said,
and I said, "You shut up devil, damned black devil from Hell."
Christophine said, "Aie Aie Aie! Look me trouble, look me cross!" '

After a long time I heard her say as if she were talking to herself,
10 'I have said all I want to say. I have tried to make you understand.
But nothing has changed.' She laughed.

'Don't laugh like that, Bertha.'

'My name is not Bertha; why do you call me Bertha?'

'Because it is a name I'm particularly fond of. I think of you as
15 Bertha.'

'It doesn't matter,' she said.

I said, 'When you went off this morning where did you go?'

'I went to see Christophine,' she said. 'I will tell you anything
you wish to know, but in a few words because words are no use, I
20 know that now.'

'Why did you go to see her?'

'I went to ask her to do something for me.'

'And did she do it?'

'Yes.' Another long pause.
25 'You wanted to ask her advice, was that it?'

She did not answer.

'What did she say?'

'She said that I ought to go away – to leave you.'

'Oh did she?' I said, surprised.
30 'Yes, that was her advice.'

'I want to do the best for both of us,' I said. 'So much of what
you tell me is strange, different from what I was led to expect.
Don't you feel that perhaps Christophine is right? That if you went
away from this place or I went away – exactly as you wish of course
35 – for a time, it might be the wisest thing we could do?' Then I said
sharply, 'Bertha, are you asleep, are you ill, why don't you answer

86

me?' I got up, went over to her chair and took her cold hands in mine. 'We've been sitting here long enough, it is very late.'

'You go,' she said. 'I wish to stay here in the dark . . . where I belong,' she added.

'Oh nonsense,' I said. I put my arms round her to help her up, I kissed her, but she drew away.

'Your mouth is colder than my hands,' she said. I tried to laugh. In the bedroom, I closed the shutters. 'Sleep now, we will talk things over tomorrow.'

'Yes,' she said, 'of course, but will you come in and say goodnight to me?'

'Certainly I will, my dear Bertha.'

'Not Bertha tonight,' she said.

'Of course, on this of all nights, you must be Bertha.'

'As you wish,' she said.

As I stepped into her room I noticed the white powder strewn on the floor. That was the first thing I asked her – about the powder. I asked what it was. She said it was to keep cockroaches away.

'Haven't you noticed that there are no cockroaches in this house and no centipedes? If you knew how horrible these things can be.' She had lit all the candles and the room was full of shadows. There were six on the dressing-table and three on the table near her bed. The light changed her. I had never seen her look so gay or so beautiful. She poured wine into two glasses and handed me one but I swear it was before I drank that I longed to bury my face in her hair as I used to do. I said, 'We are letting ghosts trouble us. Why shouldn't we be happy?' She said, 'Christophine knows about ghosts too, but that is not what she calls them.' She need not have done what she did to me. I will always swear that, she need not have done it. When she handed me the glass she was smiling. I remember saying in a voice that was not like my own that it was too light. I remember putting out the candles on the table near the bed and that is all I remember. All I will remember of the night.

I woke in the dark after dreaming that I was buried alive, and when I was awake the feeling of suffocation persisted. Something was lying across my mouth; hair with a sweet heavy smell. I threw it off but still I could not breathe. I shut my eyes and lay without moving for a few seconds. When I opened them I saw the candles burnt down on that abominable dressing-table, then I knew where 5 I was. The door on to the veranda was open and the breeze was so cold that I knew it must be very early in the morning, before dawn. I was cold too, deathly cold and sick and in pain. I got out of bed without looking at her, staggered into my dressing-room and saw myself in the glass. I turned away at once. I could not vomit. I only 10 retched painfully.

I thought, I have been poisoned. But it was a dull thought, like a child spelling out the letters of a word which he cannot read, and which if he could would have no meaning or context. I was too giddy to stand and fell backwards on to the bed, looking at the 15 blanket which was of a peculiar shade of yellow. After looking at it for some time I was able to go over to the window and vomit. It seemed like hours before this stopped. I would lean up against the wall and wipe my face, then the retching and sickness would start again. When it was over I lay on the bed too weak to move.

20 I have never made a greater effort in my life than I made then. I longed to lie there and sleep but forced myself up. I was weak and giddy but no longer sick or in pain. I put on my dressing-gown and splashed water on my face, then I opened the door into her room.

The cold light was on her and I looked at the sad droop of her 25 lips, the frown between her thick eyebrows, deep as if it had been cut with a knife. As I looked she moved and flung her arm out. I thought coldly, yes, very beautiful, the thin wrist, the sweet swell of the forearm, the rounded elbow, the curve of her shoulder into her upper arm. All present, all correct. As I watched, hating, her 30 face grew smooth and very young again, she even seemed to smile. A trick of the light perhaps. What else?

She may wake at any moment, I told myself. I must be quick. Her torn shift was on the floor, <u>I drew the sheet over her gently as</u> <u>if I covered a dead girl.</u> One of the glasses was empty, she had 35 drained hers. There was some wine left in the other which was on the dressing-table. I dipped my finger into it and tasted it. It was

DEATH OF THE RELATIONSHIP

➤ he treats her like a zombie after that.

bitter. I didn't look at her again, but holding the glass went on to the veranda. Hilda was there with a broom in her hand. I put my finger to my lips and she looked at me with huge eyes, then imitated me, putting her own finger to her lips.

As soon as I had dressed and got out of the house I began to run.

I do not remember that day clearly, where I ran or how I fell or wept or lay exhausted. But I found myself at last near the ruined house and the wild orange tree. Here with my head in my arms I must have slept and when I woke it was getting late and the wind was chilly. I got up and found my way back to the path which led to the house. I knew how to avoid every creeper, and I never stumbled once. I went to my dressing-room and if I passed anyone I did not see them and if they spoke I did not hear them.

There was a tray on the table with a jug of water, a glass and some brown fish cakes. I drank almost all the water, for I was very thirsty, but I did not touch the food. I sat on the bed waiting, for I knew that Amélie would come, and I knew what she would say: 'I am sorry for you.'

She came soundlessly on bare feet. 'I get you something to eat,' she said. She brought cold chicken, bread, fruit and a bottle of wine, and I drank a glass without speaking, then another. She cut some of the food up and sat beside me and fed me as if I were a child. Her arm behind my head was warm but the outside when I touched it was cool, almost cold. I looked into her lovely meaningless face, sat up and pushed the plate away. Then she said, 'I am sorry for you.'

'You've told me so before, Amélie. Is that the only song you know?'

There was a spark of gaiety in her yes, but when I laughed she put her hand over my mouth apprehensively. I pulled her down beside me and we were both laughing. That is what I remember most about that encounter. She was so gay, so natural and something of this gaiety she must have given to me, for I had not one moment of remorse. Nor was I anxious to know what was happening behind the thin partition which divided us from my wife's bedroom.

In the morning, of course, I felt differently.

Another complication. Impossible. And her skin was darker, her lips thicker than I had thought.

She was sleeping very soundly and quietly but there was aware-
ness in her eyes when she opened them, and after a moment suppressed laughter. I felt satisfied and peaceful, but not gay as she did, no, by God, not gay. I had no wish to touch her and she knew it, for she got up at once and began to dress.

'A very graceful dress,' I said and she showed me the many ways it could be worn, trailing on the floor, lifted to show a lace petticoat, or hitched up far above the knee.

I told her that I was leaving the island soon but that before I left I wanted to give her a present. It was a large present but she took it with no thanks and no expression on her face. When I asked her what she meant to do she said, 'It's long time I know what I want to do and I know I don't get it here.'

'You are beautiful enough to get anything you want,' I said.

'Yes,' she agreed simply. 'But not here.'

She wanted, it seemed, to join her sister who was a dressmaker in Demerara, but she would not stay in Demerara, she said. She wanted to go to Rio. There were rich men in Rio.

'And when will you start all this?' I said, amused.

'I start now.' She would catch one of the fishing boats at Massacre and get into town.

I laughed and teased her. She was running away from the old woman Christophine, I said.

She was unsmiling when she answered, 'I have malice to no one but I don't stay here.'

I asked her how she would get to Massacre. 'I don't want no horse or mule,' she said. 'My legs strong enough to carry me.'

As she was going I could not resist saying, half longing, half triumphant, 'Well, Amélie, are you still sorry for me?'

'Yes,' she said, 'I am sorry for you. But I find it in my heart to be sorry for her too.'

She shut the door gently. I lay and listened for the sound I knew I should hear, the horse's hoofs as my wife left the house.

I turned over and slept till Baptiste woke me with coffee. His face was gloomy.

'The cook is leaving,' he announced.

'Why?'

He shrugged his shoulders and spread his hands open. 5

I got up, looked out of the window and saw her stride out of the kitchen, a strapping woman. She couldn't speak English, or said she couldn't. I forgot this when I said, 'I must talk to her. What is the huge bundle on her head?'

'Her mattress,' said Baptiste. 'She will come back for the rest. 10 No good to talk to her. She won't stay in this house.'

I laughed.

'Are you leaving too?'

'No,' said Baptiste. 'I am overseer here.'

I noticed that he did not call me 'sir' or 'master'. 15

'And the little girl, Hilda?'

'Hilda will do as I tell her. Hilda will stay.'

'Capital,' I said. 'Then why are you looking so anxious? Your mistress will be back soon.'

He shrugged again and muttered, but whether he was talking 20 about my morals or the extra work he would have to do I couldn't tell, for he muttered in patois.

I told him to sling one of the veranda hammocks under the cedar trees and there I spent the rest of that day.

Baptiste provided meals, but he seldom smiled and never 25 spoke except to answer a question. My wife did not return. Yet I was not lonely or unhappy. Sun, sleep and the cool water of the river were enough. I wrote a cautious letter to Mr Fraser on the third day.

I told him that I was considering a book about obeah and had 30 remembered his story of the case he had come across. Had he any idea of the whereabouts of the woman now? Was she still in Jamaica?

This letter was sent down by the twice weekly messenger and he must have answered at once for I had his reply in a few days: 35

I have often thought of your wife and yourself. And was on the point of writing to you. Indeed I have not forgotten the case. The woman in question was called Josephine or Christophine Dubois, some such name and she had been one of the Cosway servants. After she came out of jail she dis-
5 appeared, but it was common knowledge that old Mr Mason befriended her. I heard that she owned or was given a small house and a piece of land near Granbois. She is intelligent in her way and can express herself well, but I did not like the look of her at all, and consider her a most dangerous person. My wife insisted that she had gone back to Martinique her native
10 island, and was very upset that I had mentioned the matter even in such a roundabout fashion. I happen to know now that she has not returned to Martinique, so I have written very discreetly to Hill, the white inspector of police in your town. If she lives near you and gets up to any of her nonsense let him know at once. He'll send a couple of policemen up to
15 your place and she won't get off lightly this time. I'll make sure of that. . . .

So much for you, Josephine or Christophine, I thought. So much for you, Pheena.

It was that half-hour after the sunset, the blue half-hour I called it to myself. The wind drops, the light is very beautiful, the mountains
20 sharp, every leaf on every tree is clear and distinct. I was sitting in the hammock, watching, when Antoinette rode up. She passed me without looking at me, dismounted and went into the house. I heard her bedroom door slam and her handbell ring violently. Baptiste came running along the veranda. I got out of the hammock
25 and went to the sitting-room. He had opened the chest and taken out a bottle of rum. Some of this he poured into a decanter which he put on a tray with a glass.

'Who is that for?' I said. He didn't answer.

'No road?' I said and laughed.
30 'I don't want to know nothing about all this,' he said.

'Baptiste!' Antoinette called in a high voice.

'Yes, mistress.' He looked straight at me and carried the tray out.

As for the old woman, I saw her shadow before I saw her. She too passed me without turning her head. Nor did she go into

Antoinette's room or look towards it. She walked along the veranda, down the steps the other side, and went into the kitchen. In that short time the dark had come and Hilda came in to light the candles. When I spoke to her she gave me an alarmed look and ran away. I opened the chest and looked at the rows of bottles 5 inside. Here was the rum that kills you in a hundred years, the brandy, the red and white wine smuggled, I suppose, from St Pierre, Martinique – the Paris of the West Indies. It was rum I chose to drink. Yes, it was mild in the mouth, I waited a second for the explosion of heat and light in my chest, the strength and warmth 10 running through my body. Then I tried the door into Antoinette's room. It yielded very slightly. She must have pushed some piece of furniture against it, that round table probably. I pushed again and it opened enough for me to see her. She was lying on the bed on her back. Her eyes were closed and she breathed heavily. She had 15 pulled the sheet up to her chin. On a chair beside the bed there was the empty decanter, a glass with some rum left in it and a small brass handbell.

I shut the door and sat down with my elbows on the table for I thought I knew what would happen and what I must do. I found 20 the room oppressively hot, so I blew out most of the candles and waited in the half darkness. Then I went on to the veranda to watch the door of the kitchen where a light was showing.

Soon the little girl came out followed by Baptiste. At the same time the handbell in the bedroom rang. They both went into the 25 sitting-room and I followed. Hilda lit all the candles with a frightened roll of the eyes in my direction. The handbell went on ringing.

'Mix me a good strong one, Baptiste. Just what I feel like.'

He took a step away from me and said, 'Miss Antoinette –'

'Baptiste, where are you?' Antoinette called. 'Why don't you 30 come?'

'I come as quick as I can,' Baptiste said. But as he reached for the bottle I took it away from him.

Hilda ran out of the room. Baptiste and I stared at each other. I thought that his large protuberant eyes and his expression of utter 35 bewilderment were comical.

Antoinette shrieked from the bedroom, 'Baptiste! Christophine! Pheena, Pheena!'

'*Que komesse!*' Baptiste said. 'I get Christophine.'

He ran out almost as fast as the little girl had done.

5   The door of Antoinette's room opened. When I saw her I was too shocked to speak. Her hair hung uncombed and dull into her eyes which were inflamed and staring, her face was very flushed and looked swollen. Her feet were bare. However when she spoke her voice was low, almost inaudible.

10   'I rang the bell because I was thirsty. Didn't anybody hear?'

Before I could stop her she darted to the table and seized the bottle of rum.

'Don't drink any more,' I said.

'And what right have you to tell me what I'm to do? 15 Christophine!' she called again, but her voice broke.

'Christophine is an evil old woman and you know it as well as I do,' I said. 'She won't stay here very much longer.'

'She won't stay here very much longer,' she mimicked me, 'and nor will you, nor will you. I thought you liked the black people so 20 much,' she said, still in that mincing voice, 'but that's just a lie like everything else. You like the light brown girls better, don't you? You abused the planters and made up stories about them, but you do the same thing. You send the girl away quicker, and with no money or less money, and that's all the difference.'

25   'Slavery was not a matter of liking or disliking,' I said, trying to speak calmly. 'It was a question of justice.'

'Justice,' she said. 'I've heard that word. It's a cold word. I tried it out,' she said, still speaking in a low voice. 'I wrote it down. I wrote it down several times and always it looked like a damn cold 30 lie to me. There is no justice.' She drank some more rum and went on, 'My mother whom you all talk about, what justice did she have? My mother sitting in the rocking-chair speaking about dead horses and dead grooms and a black devil kissing her sad mouth. Like you kissed mine,' she said.

35   The room was now unbearably hot. 'I'll open the window and let a little air in,' I said.

'It will let the night in too,' she said, 'and the moon and the scent of those flowers you dislike so much.'

When I turned from the window she was drinking again.

'Bertha,' I said.

'Bertha is not my name. You are trying to make me into someone else, calling me by another name. I know, that's obeah too.'

Tears streamed from her eyes.

'If my father, my real father, was alive you wouldn't come back here in a hurry after he'd finished with you. If he was alive. Do you know what you've done to me? It's not the girl, not the girl. But I loved this place and you have made it into a place I hate. I used to think that if everything else went out of my life I would still have this, and now you have spoilt it. It's just somewhere else where I have been unhappy, and all the other things are nothing to what has happened here. I hate it now like I hate you and before I die I will show you how much I hate you.'

Then to my astonishment she stopped crying and said, 'Is she so much prettier than I am? Don't you love me at all?'

'No, I do not,' I said (at the same time remembering Amélie saying, 'Do you like my hair? Isn't it prettier than hers?'). 'Not at this moment,' I said.

She laughed at that. A crazy laugh.

'You see. That's how you are. A stone. But it serves me right because didn't Aunt Cora say to me don't marry him. Not if he were stuffed with diamonds. And a lot of other things she told me. Are you talking about England, I said, and what about Grandpappy passing his glass over the water decanter and the tears running down his face for all the friends dead and gone, whom he would never see again. That was nothing to do with England that I ever heard, she said. On the contrary:

> A Benky foot and a Benky leg
> For Charlie over the water.
> Charlie, Charlie,'

she sang in a hoarse voice. And lifted the bottle to drink again.

I said, and my voice was not very calm, 'No.'

I managed to hold her wrist with one hand and the rum with the other, but when I felt her teeth in my arm I dropped the bottle. The smell filled the room. But I was angry now and she saw it. She smashed another bottle against the wall and stood with the broken
5 glass in her hand and murder in her eyes.

'Just you touch me once. You'll soon see if I'm a dam' coward like you are.'

Then she cursed me comprehensively, my eyes, my mouth, every member of my body, and it was like a dream in the large unfurnished
10 room with the candles flickering and this red-eyed wild-haired stranger who was my wife shouting obscenities at me. It was at this nightmare moment that I heard Christophine's calm voice.

'You hush up and keep yourself quiet. And don't cry. Crying's no good with him. I told you before. Crying's no good.'

15 Antoinette collapsed on the sofa and went on sobbing. Christophine looked at me and her small eyes were very sad. 'Why you do that eh? Why you don't take that worthless good-for-nothing girl somewhere else? But she love money like you love money – must be why you come together. Like goes to like.'

20 I couldn't bear any more and again I went out of the room and sat on the veranda.

My arm was bleeding and painful and I wrapped my hand-kerchief round it, but it seemed to me that everything round me was hostile. The telescope drew away and said don't touch me.
25 The trees were threatening and the shadows of the trees moving slowly over the floor menaced me. That green menace. I had felt it ever since I saw this place. There was nothing I knew, nothing to comfort me.

I listened. Christophine was talking softly. My wife was crying.
30 Then a door shut. They had gone into the bedroom. Someone was singing '*Ma belle ka di*', or was it the song about one day and a thousand years? But whatever they were singing or saying was dangerous. I must protect myself. I went softly along the dark veranda. I could see Antoinette stretched on the bed quite still.
35 Like a doll. Even when she threatened me with the bottle she had a marionette quality. '*Ti moun*,' I heard and '*Doudou ché*,' and the

end of a head handkerchief made a finger on the wall. '*Do do l'enfant do*.' Listening, I began to feel sleepy and cold.

I stumbled back into the big candlelit room which still smelt strongly of rum. In spite of this I opened the chest and got out another bottle. That was what I was thinking when Christophine 5 came in. I was thinking of a last strong drink in my room, fastening both doors, and sleeping.

'I hope you satisfy, I hope you well satisfy,' she said, 'and no good to start your lies with me. I know what you do with that girl as well as you know. Better. Don't think I frightened of you either.' 10

'So she ran off to tell you I'd ill-treated her, did she? I ought to have guessed that.'

'She don't tell me a thing,' said Christophine. 'Not one single thing. Always the same. Nobody is to have any pride but you. She have more pride than you and she say nothing. I see her standing 15 at my door with that look on her face and I know something bad happen to her. I know I must act quick and I act.'

'You seem to have acted, certainly. And what did you do before you brought her back in her present condition?'

'What did I do! Look! don't you provoke me more than I provoke 20 already. Better not I tell you. You want to know what I do? I say *doudou*, if you have trouble you are right to come to me. And I kiss her. It's when I kiss her she cry – not before. It's long time she hold it back, I think. So I let her cry. That is the first thing. Let them cry – it eases the heart. When she can't cry no more I give her a 25 cup of milk – it's lucky I have some. She won't eat, she won't talk. So I say, "Lie down on the bed *doudou* and try to sleep, for me I can sleep on the floor, don't matter for me." She isn't going to sleep natural that's certain, but I can make her sleep. That's what I do. As for what you do – you pay for it one day. 30

'When they get like that,' she said, 'first they must cry, then they must sleep. Don't talk to me about doctor, I know more than any doctor. I undress Antoinette so she can sleep cool and easy; it's then I see you very rough with her eh?'

At this point she laughed – a hearty merry laugh. 'All that is a 35 little thing – it's nothing. If you see what I see in this place with the machete bright and shining in the corner, you don't have such a long face for such a little thing. You make her love you more if that's what you want. It's not for that she have the look of death on her face. Oh no.

5   'One night,' she went on, 'I hold on a woman's nose because her husband nearly chop it off with his machete. I hold it on, I send a boy running for the doctor and the doctor come galloping at dead of night to sew up the woman. When he finish he tell me, "Christophine you have a great presence of mind." That's what

10 he tell me. By this time the man crying like a baby. He says, "Doctor I don't mean it. It just happened." "I know, Rupert," the doctor says, "but it mustn't happen again. Why don't you keep the damn machete in the other room?" he says. They have two small rooms only so I say, "No, doctor – it much worse near the bed.

15 They chop each other up in no time at all." The doctor he laugh and laugh. Oh he was a good doctor. When he finished with that woman nose I won't say it look like before but I will say it don't notice much. Rupert that man's name was. Plenty Ruperts here you notice? One is Prince Rupert, and one who makes songs is

20 Rupert the Rine. You see him? He sells his songs down by the bridge there in town. It's in the town I live when I first leave Jamaica. It's a pretty name eh – Rupert – but where they get it from? I think it's from old time they get it.

   'That doctor an old-time doctor. These new ones I don't like

25 them. First word in their mouth is police. Police – that's something I don't like.'

   'I'm sure you don't,' I said. 'But you haven't told me yet what happened when my wife was with you. Or exactly what you did?'

   '*Your wife!*' she said. 'You make me laugh. I don't know all you

30 did but I know some. Everybody know that you marry her for her money and you take it all. And then you want to break her up, because you jealous of her. She is more better than you, she have better blood in her and she don't care for money – it's nothing for her. Oh I see that first time I look at you. You young but already

35 you hard. You fool the girl. You make her think you can't see the sun for looking at her.'

It was like that, I thought. It was like that. But better to say nothing. Then surely they'll both go and it will be my turn to sleep – a long deep sleep, mine will be, and very far away.

'And then,' she went on in her judge's voice, 'you make love to her till she drunk with it, no rum could make her drunk like that, till she can't do without it. It's *she* can't see the sun any more. Only you she see. But all you want is to break her up.'

(*Not the way you mean, I thought*)

'But she hold out eh? She hold out.'

(*Yes, she held out. A pity*)

'So you pretend to believe all the lies that damn bastard tell you.'

(*That damn bastard tell you*)

Now every word she said was echoed, echoed loudly in my head.

'So that you can leave her alone.'

(*Leave her alone*)

'Not telling her why.'

(*Why?*)

'No more love, eh?'

(*No more love*)

'And that,' I said coldly, 'is where you took charge, isn't it? You tried to poison me.'

'Poison you? But look me trouble, the man crazy! She come to me and ask me for something to make you love her again and I tell her no I don't meddle in that for *béké*. I tell her it's foolishness.'

(*Foolishness foolishness*)

'And even if it's no foolishness, it's too strong for *béké*.'

(*Too strong for* béké. *Too strong*)

'But she cry and she beg me.'

(*She cry and she beg me*)

'So I give her something for love.'

(*For love*)

'But you don't love. All you want is to break her up. And it help you break her up.'

(*Break her up*)

'She tell me in the middle of all this you start calling her names. Marionette. Some word so.'

'Yes, I remember, I did.'

(*Marionette, Antoinette, Marionetta, Antoinetta*)

'That word mean doll, eh? Because she don't speak. You want to force her to cry and to speak.'

5   (*Force her to cry and to speak*)

'But she won't. So you think up something else. You bring that worthless girl to play with next door and you talk and laugh and love so that she hear everything. You meant her to hear.'

Yes, that didn't just happen. I meant it.

10   (*I lay awake all night long after they were asleep, and as soon as it was light I got up and dressed and saddled Preston. And I came to you. Oh Christophine. O Pheena, Pheena, help me.*)

'You haven't yet told me exactly what you did with my – with Antoinette.'

15   'Yes I tell you. I make her sleep.'

'What? All the time?'

'No, no. I wake her up to sit in the sun, bathe in the cool river. Even if she dropping with sleep. I make good strong soup. I give her milk if I have it, fruit I pick from my own trees. If she don't
20 want to eat I say, "Eat it up for my sake, *doudou*." And she eat it up, then she sleep again.'

'And why did you do all this?'

There was a long silence. Then she said, 'It's better she sleep. She must sleep while I work for her – to make her well again. But
25 I don't speak of all that to you.'

'Unfortunately your cure was not successful. You didn't make her well. You made her worse.'

'Yes I succeed,' she said angrily. 'I succeed. But I get frightened that she sleep too much, too long. She is not *béké*, like you, but she
30 is *béké*, and not like us either. There are mornings when she can't wake, or when she wake it's as if she still sleeping. I don't want to give her any more of – of what I give. So,' she went on after another pause, 'I let her have rum instead. I know that won't hurt her. Not much. As soon as she has the rum she starts raving that she must
35 go back to you and I can't quiet her. She says she'll go alone if I don't come but she beg me to come. And I hear well when you tell

her that you don't love her – quite calm and cool you tell her so, and undo all the good I do.'

'The good you did! I'm very weary of your nonsense, Christophine. You seem to have made her dead drunk on bad rum and she's a wreck. I scarcely recognized her. Why you did it I can't say 5 – hatred of me I suppose. And as you heard so much perhaps you were listening to all she admitted – boasted about, and to the vile names she called me. Your *doudou* certainly knows some filthy language.'

'I tell you no. I tell you it's nothing. You make her so unhappy 10 she don't know what she is saying. Her father old Mister Cosway swear like half past midnight – she pick it up from him. And once, when she was little she run away to be with the fishermen and the sailors on the bayside. Those men!' She raised her eyes to the ceiling. 'Never would you think they was once innocent babies. 15 She come back copying them. She don't understand what she says.'

'I think she understood every word, and meant what she said too. But you are right, Christophine – it was all a very little thing. It was nothing. No machete here, so no machete damage. No 20 damage at all by this time. I'm sure you took care of that however drunk you made her.'

'You are a damn hard man for a young man.'

'So you say, so you say.'

'I tell her so. I warn her. I say this is not a man who will help you 25 when he sees you break up. Only the best can do that. The best – and sometimes the worst.'

'But you think I'm one of the worst, surely?'

'No,' she said indifferently, 'to me you are not the best, not the worst. You are –' she shrugged ' – you will not help her. I tell her so.' 30

Nearly all the candles were out. She didn't light fresh ones – nor did I. We sat in the dim light. I should stop this useless conversation, I thought, but could only listen, hypnotized, to her dark voice coming from the darkness.

'I know that girl. She will never ask you for love again, she will 35 die first. But I Christophine I beg you. She love you so much. She

thirsty for you. Wait, and perhaps you can love her again. A little,
like she say. A little. Like you can love.'

I shook my head and went on shaking it mechanically.

'It's lies all that yellow bastard tell you. He is no Cosway either.
5 His mother was a no-good woman and she try to fool the old man
but the old man isn't fooled. "One more or less," he says, and
laughs. He was wrong. More he do for those people, more they
hate him. The hate in that man Daniel – he can't rest with it. If I
know you coming here I stop you. But you marry quick, you leave
10 Jamaica quick. No time.'

'She told me that all he said was true. She wasn't lying then.'

'Because you hurt her she want to hurt you back, that's why.'

'And that her mother was mad. Another lie?'

Christophine did not answer me at once. When she did her voice
15 was not so calm.

'They drive her to it. When she lose her son she lose herself for
a while and they shut her away. They tell her she is mad, they act
like she is mad. Question, question. But no kind word, no friends,
and her husban' he go off, he leave her. They won't let me see her.
20 I try, but no. They won't let Antoinette see her. In the end – mad
I don't know – she give up, she care for nothing. That man who is
in charge of her he take her whenever he want and his woman talk.
That man, and others. Then they have her. Ah there is no God.'

'Only your spirits,' I reminded her.

25 'Only my spirits,' she said steadily. 'In your Bible it say God is a
spirit – it don't say no others. Not at all. It grieve me what happen to
her mother, and I can't see it happen again. You call her a doll? She
don't satisfy you? Try her once more, I think she satisfy you now. If
you forsake her they will tear her in pieces – like they did her mother.'

30 'I will not forsake her,' I said wearily. 'I will do all I can for her.'

'You will love her like you did before?'

(*Give my sister your wife a kiss from me. Love her as I did – oh yes I
did. How can I promise that?*) I said nothing.

'It's she won't be satisfy. She is Creole girl, and she have the sun
35 in her. Tell the truth now. She don't come to your house in this place
England they tell me about, she don't come to your beautiful house

to beg you to marry with her. No, it's you come all the long way to her house – it's you beg her to marry. And she love you and she give you all she have. Now you say you don't love her and you break her up. What you do with her money, eh?' Her voice was still quiet but with a hiss in it when she said 'money'. I thought, of course, that is 5 what all the rigmarole is about. I no longer felt dazed, tired, half hypnotized, but alert and wary, ready to defend myself.

Why, she wanted to know, could I not return half of Antoinette's dowry and leave the island – 'leave the West Indies if you don't want her no more.' 10

I asked the exact sum she had in mind, but she was vague about that.

'You fix it up with lawyers and all those things.'

'And what will happen to her then?'

She, Christophine, would take good care of Antoinette (and the 15 money of course).

'You will both stay here?' I hoped that my voice was as smooth as hers.

No, they would go to Martinique. Then to other places.

'I like to see the world before I die.' 20

Perhaps because I was so quiet and composed she added maliciously, 'She marry with someone else. She forget about you and live happy.'

A pang of rage and jealousy shot through me then. Oh no, she won't forget. I laughed. 25

'You laugh at me? Why you laugh at me?'

'Of course I laugh at you – you ridiculous old woman. I don't mean to discuss my affairs with you any longer. Or your mistress. I've listened to all you had to say and I don't believe you. Now, say good-bye to Antoinette, then go. You are to blame for all that has 30 happened here, so don't come back.'

She drew herself up tall and straight and put her hands on her hips. 'Who you to tell me to go? This house belong to Miss Antoinette's mother, now it belong to her. Who you to tell me to go?'

'I assure you that it belongs to me now. You'll go, or I'll get the 35 men to put you out.'

'You think the men here touch me? They not damn fool like you to put their hand on me.'

'Then I will have the police up, I warn you. There must be some law and order even in this God-forsaken island.'

5 'No police here,' she said. 'No chain gang, no tread machine, no dark jail either. This is free country and I am free woman.'

[margin note: Rochester taking the voice of someone else to exert power over.]

'Christophine,' I said, 'you lived in Jamaica for years, and you know Mr Fraser, the Spanish Town magistrate, well. I wrote to him about you. Would you like to hear what he answered?' She
10 stared at me. I read the end of Fraser's letter aloud: '*I have written very discreetly to Hill, the white inspector of police in your town. If she lives near you and gets up to any of her nonsense let him know at once. He'll send a couple of policemen up to your place and she won't get off lightly this time. . . . .* You gave your mistress the poison that she put
15 into my wine?'

'I tell you already – you talk foolishness.'

'We'll see about that – I kept some of that wine.'

'I tell her so,' she said. 'Always it don't work for *béké*. Always it bring trouble . . . So you send me away and you keep all her money.
20 And what you do with her?'

'I don't see why I should tell you my plans. I mean to go back to Jamaica to consult the Spanish Town doctors and her brother. I'll follow their advice. That is all I mean to do. She is not well.'

'Her brother!' She spat on the floor. 'Richard Mason is no
25 brother to her. You think you fool me? You want her money but you don't want her. It is in your mind to pretend she is mad. I know it. The doctors say what you tell them to say. That man Richard he say what you want him to say – glad and willing too, I know. She will be like her mother. You do that for money? But you
30 wicked like Satan self!'

I said loudly and wildly, 'And do you think that I wanted all this? I would give my life to undo it. I would give my eyes never to have seen this abominable place.'

She laughed. 'And that's the first damn word of truth you speak.
35 You choose what you give, eh? Then you choose. You meddle in something and perhaps you don't know what it is.' She began to

mutter to herself. Not in patois. I knew the sound of patois now.

She's as mad as the other, I thought, and turned to the window.

The servants were standing in a group under the clove tree. Baptiste, the boy who helped with the horses and the little girl Hilda.

Christophine was right. They didn't intend to get mixed up in this business.

When I looked at her there was a mask on her face and her eyes were undaunted. She was a fighter, I had to admit. Against my will I repeated, 'Do you wish to say good-bye to Antoinette?'

'I give her something to sleep – nothing to hurt her. I don't wake her up to no misery. I leave that for you.'

'You can write to her,' I said stiffly.

'Read and write I don't know. Other things I know.'

She walked away without looking back. *her sense of being/base of power comes from a different place than Rochester*

All wish to sleep had left me. I walked up and down the room and felt the blood tingle in my finger-tips. It ran up my arms and reached my heart, which began to beat very fast. I spoke aloud as I walked. I spoke the letter I meant to write.

'I know now that you planned this because you wanted to be rid of me. You had no love at all for me. Nor had my brother. Your plan succeeded because I was young, conceited, foolish, trusting. Above all because I was young. You were able to do this to me . . .'

But I am not young now, I thought, stopped pacing and drank. Indeed this rum is mild as mother's milk or father's blessing.

I could imagine his expression if I sent that letter and he read it.

I wrote

Dear Father,

We are leaving this island for Jamaica very shortly. Unforeseen circumstances, at least unforeseen by me, have forced me to make this decision. I am certain that you know or can guess what has happened, and I am certain you will believe that the less you talk to anyone about my affairs, especially my marriage, the better. This is in your interest as well as mine. You will hear from me again. Soon I hope.

Then I wrote to the firm of lawyers I had dealt with in Spanish Town. I told them that I wished to rent a furnished house not too near the town, commodious enough to allow for two separate suites of rooms. I also told them to engage a staff of servants whom I was
5 prepared to pay very liberally – so long as they keep their mouths shut, I thought – provided that they are discreet, I wrote. My wife and myself would be in Jamaica in about a week and expected to find everything ready.

All the time I was writing this letter a cock crowed persistently
10 outside. I took the first book I could lay hands on and threw it at him, but he stalked a few yards away and started again.

Baptiste appeared, looking towards Antoinette's silent room.

'Have you got much more of this famous rum?'

'Plenty rum,' he said.
15 'Is it really a hundred years old?'

He nodded indifferently. A hundred years, a thousand all the same to *le bon Dieu* and Baptiste too.

'What's that damn cock crowing about?'

'Crowing for change of weather.'
20 Because his eyes were fixed on the bedroom I shouted at him, 'Asleep, *dormi, dormi.*'

He shook his head and went away.

He scowled at me then, I thought. I scowled too as I re-read the letter I had written to the lawyers. However much I paid Jamaican
25 servants I would never buy discretion. I'd be gossiped about, sung about (but they make up songs about everything, everybody. You should hear the one about the Governor's wife). Wherever I went I would be talked about. I drank some more rum and, drinking, I drew a house surrounded by trees. A large house. I divided the
30 third floor into rooms and in one room I drew a standing woman – a child's scribble, a dot for a head, a larger one for the body, a triangle for a skirt, slanting lines for arms and feet. But it was an English house.

English trees. I wondered if I ever should see England again.

*

Under the oleanders . . . I watched the hidden mountains and the mists drawn over their faces. It's cool today; cool, calm and cloudy as an English summer. But a lovely place in any weather, however far I travel I'll never see a lovelier.

The hurricane months are not so far away, I thought, and saw that tree strike its roots deeper, making ready to fight the wind. Useless. If and when it comes they'll all go. Some of the royal 5 palms stand (she told me). Stripped of their branches, like tall brown pillars, still they stand – defiant. Not for nothing are they called royal. The bamboos take an easier way, they bend to the earth and lie there, creaking, groaning, crying for mercy. The contemptuous wind passes, not caring for these abject things. (*Let* 10 *them live*.) Howling, shrieking, laughing the wild blast passes.

But all that's some months away. It's an English summer now, so cool, so grey. Yet I think of my revenge and hurricanes. Words rush through my head (deeds too). Words. Pity is one of them. It gives me no rest. ~~quote from Macbeth. Rochester becomes cold and 15 unfeeling like~~
" Pity like a naked new-born babe striding the blast." ~~a Macbeth character.~~
I read that long ago when I was young – I hate poets now and poetry. As I hate music which I loved once. Sing your songs, Rupert the Rine, but I'll not listen, though they tell me you've a sweet voice. . . . 20

Pity. Is there none for me? Tied to a lunatic for life – a drunken lying lunatic – gone her mother's way.

'*She love you so much, so much. She thirsty for you. Love her a little like she say. It's all that you can love – a little.*'

Sneer to the last, Devil. Do you think that I don't know? She 25 thirsts for *anyone* – not for me . . .

She'll loosen her black hair, and laugh and coax and flatter (a mad girl. She'll not care who she's loving.) She'll moan and cry and give herself as no sane woman would – or could. *Or could.* Then lie so still, still as this cloudy day. A lunatic who always knows 30 the time. But never does.

Till she's drunk so deep, played her games so often that the lowest shrug and jeer at her. And I'm to know it – I? No, I've a trick worth two of that.

'*She love you so much, so much. Try her once more.*'

I tell you she loves no one, anyone. I could not touch her. Excepting as the hurricane will touch that tree – and break it. You say I did? No. That was love's fierce play. Now I'll do it.

5 She'll not laugh in the sun again. She'll not dress up and smile at herself in that damnable looking-glass. So pleased, so satisfied.

Vain, silly creature. Made for loving? Yes, but she'll have no lover, for I don't want her and she'll see no other.

The tree shivers. Shivers and gathers all its strength. And waits.

10 (There is a cool wind blowing now – a cold wind. Does it carry the babe born to stride the blast of hurricanes?)

She said she loved this place. This is the last she'll see of it. I'll watch for one tear, one human tear. Not that blank hating moonstruck face. I'll listen. . . . If she says good-bye perhaps adieu.

15 *Adieu* – like those old-time songs she sang. Always *adieu* (and all songs say it). If she too says it, or weeps, I'll take her in my arms, my lunatic. She's mad but *mine, mine*. What will I care for gods or devils or for Fate itself. If she smiles or weeps or both. *For me.*

Antoinetta – I can be gentle too. Hide your face. Hide yourself
20 but in my arms. You'll soon see how gentle. My lunatic. My mad girl.

Here's a cloudy day to help you. No brazen sun.

No sun . . . No sun. The weather's changed.

Sun imagery = Antoinette having identity
↳ Rochester has taken Antoinette's identity away.

Baptiste was waiting and the horses saddled. That boy stood by
25 the clove tree and near him the basket he was to carry. These baskets are light and waterproof. I'd decided to use one for a few necessary clothes – most of our belongings were to follow in a day or two. A carriage was to meet us at Massacre. I'd seen to everything, arranged everything.

She was there in the *ajoupa*; carefully dressed for the journey, I noticed, but her face blank, no expression at all. Tears? There's
30 not a tear in her. Well, we will see. Did she remember anything, I wondered, feel anything? (That blue cloud, that shadow, is Martinique. It's clear now . . . Or the names of the mountains. No, not

mountain. *Morne,* she'd say. 'Mountain is an ugly word – for them.'
Or the stories about Jack Spaniards. Long ago. And when she said,
'Look! The Emerald Drop! That brings good fortune.' Yes, for a
moment the sky was green – a bright green sunset. Strange. But
not half so strange as saying it brought good fortune.)   5

After all I was prepared for her blank indifference. I knew that
my dreams were dreams. But the sadness I felt looking at the
shabby white house – I wasn't prepared for that. More than ever
before it strained away from the black snake-like forest. Louder
and more desperately it called: Save me from destruction, ruin and   10
desolation. Save me from the long slow death by ants. But what
are you doing here you folly? So near the forest. Don't you know
that this is a dangerous place? And that the dark forest always wins?
Always. If you don't, you soon will, and I can do nothing to help
you.   15

Baptiste looked very different. Not a trace of the polite domestic.
He wore a very wide-brimmed straw hat, like the fishermen's hats,
but the crown flat, not high and pointed. His wide leather belt was
polished, so was the handle of his sheathed cutlass, and his blue
cotton shirt and trousers were spotless. The hat, I knew, was   20
waterproof. He was ready for the rain and it was certainly on its
way.

I said that I would like to say good-bye to the little girl who
laughed – Hilda. 'Hilda is not here,' he answered in his careful
English. 'Hilda has left – yesterday.'   25

He spoke politely enough, but I could feel his dislike and contempt. The same contempt as that devil's when she said, 'Taste
my bull's blood.' Meaning that will make you a man. Perhaps.
Much I cared for what they thought of me! As for her, I'd forgotten
her for the moment. So I shall never understand why, suddenly,   30
bewilderingly, I was certain that everything I had imagined to be
truth was false. False. Only the magic and the dream are true – all
the rest's a lie. Let it go. Here is the secret. Here.

(*But it is lost, that secret, and those who know it cannot tell it.*)

Not lost. I had found it in a hidden place and I'd keep it, hold it   35
fast. As I'd hold her.

I looked at her. She was staring out to the distant sea. She was silence itself.

Sing, Antoinetta. I can hear you now.

<pre>
        Here the wind says it has been, it has been
5   And the sea says it must be, it must be
        And the sun says it can be, it will be
        And the rain . . . ?
</pre>

'*You must listen to that. Our rain knows all the songs.*'
'*And all the tears?*'
10   '*All, all, all.*'

Yes, I will listen to the rain. I will listen to the mountain bird. Oh, a heartstopper is the solitaire's one note – high, sweet, lonely, magic. You hold your breath to listen . . . No . . . Gone. What was I to say to her?

15   Do not be sad. Or think Adieu. Never Adieu. We will watch the sun set again – many times, and perhaps we'll see the Emerald Drop, the green flash that brings good fortune. And you must laugh and chatter as you used to do – telling me about the battle off the Saints or the picnic at Marie Galante – that famous picnic
20   that turned into a fight. Or the pirates and what they did between voyages. For every voyage might be their last. Sun and sangoree's a heady mixture. Then – the earthquake. Oh yes, people say that God was angry at the things they did, woke from his sleep, one breath and they were gone. He slept again. But they left their
25   treasure, gold and more than gold. Some of it is found – but the finders never tell, because you see they'd only get one-third then: that's the law of treasure. They want it all, so never speak of it. Sometimes precious things, or jewels. There's no end to what they find and sell in secret to some cautious man who weighs and
30   measures, hesitates, asks questions which are not answered, then hands over money in exchange. Everybody knows that gold pieces, treasures, appear in Spanish Town – (here too). In all the islands, from nowhere, from no one knows where. For it is better not to speak of treasure. Better not to tell them.

35   Yes, better not to tell them. I won't tell you that I scarcely

listened to your stories. I was longing for night and darkness and the time when the moonflowers open.

> Blot out the moon,
> Pull down the stars.
> Love in the dark, for we're for the dark 5
> So soon, so soon.

Like the swaggering pirates, let's make the most and best and worst of what we have. Give not one-third but everything. All – all – all. Keep nothing back. . . .

No, I would say – I knew what I would say. 'I have made a 10 terrible mistake. Forgive me.'

I said it, looking at her, seeing the hatred in her eyes – and feeling my own hate spring up to meet it. Again the giddy change, the remembering, the sickening swing back to hate. They bought me, *me* with your paltry money. You helped them to do it. You deceived 15 me, betrayed me, and you'll do worse if you get the chance . . . (*That girl she look you straight in the eye and talk sweet talk – and it's lies she tell you. Lies. Her mother was so. They say she worse than her mother.*)

. . . If I was bound for hell let it be hell. No more false heavens. No more damned magic. You hate me and I hate you. We'll see 20 who hates best. But first, first I will destroy your hatred. Now. My hate is colder, stronger, and you'll have no hate to warm yourself. You will have nothing. ~~made her into a zombie~~

I did it too. I saw the hate go out of her eyes. I forced it out. And with the hate her beauty. She was only a ghost. A ghost in the grey 25 daylight. Nothing left but hopelessness. *Say die and I will die. Say die and watch me die.*

She lifted her eyes. Blank lovely eyes. Mad eyes. A mad girl. I don't know what I would have said or done. In the balance – everything. But at this moment the nameless boy leaned his head 30 against the clove tree and sobbed. Loud heartbreaking sobs. I could have strangled him with pleasure. But I managed to control myself, walk up to them and say coldly, 'What is the matter with him? What is he crying about?' Baptiste did not answer. His sullen face grew a shade more sullen and that was all I got from Baptiste. 35

She had followed me and she answered. I scarcely recognized her voice. No warmth, no sweetness. The doll had a doll's voice, a breathless but curiously indifferent voice.

'He asked me when we first came if we – if you – would take him
5 with you when we left. He doesn't want any money. Just to be with you. Because –' she stopped and ran her tongue over her lips, 'he loves you very much. So I said you would. Take him. Baptiste has told him that you will not. So he is crying.'

'I certainly will not,' I said angrily. (God! A half-savage boy as
10 well as . . . as well as . . .)

'He knows English,' she said, still indifferently. 'He has tried very hard to learn English.'

'He hasn't learned any English that I can understand,' I said. And looking at her stiff white face my fury grew. 'What right have
15 you to make promises in my name? Or to speak for me at all?'

'No, I had no right, I am sorry. I don't understand you. I know nothing about you, and I cannot speak for you. . . .'

And that was all. I said good-bye to Baptiste. He bowed stiffly, unwillingly and muttered – wishes for a pleasant journey, I suppose.
20 He hoped, I am sure, that he'd never set eyes on me again.

She had mounted and he went over to her. When she stretched her hand out he took it and still holding it spoke to her very earnestly. I did not hear what he said but I thought she would cry then. No, the doll's smile came back – nailed to her face. Even if
25 she had wept like Magdalene it would have made no difference. I was exhausted. All the mad conflicting emotions had gone and left me wearied and empty. Sane.

I was tired of these people. I disliked their laughter and their tears, their flattery and envy, conceit and deceit. And I hated the place.
30 I hated the mountains and the hills, the rivers and the rain. I hated the sunsets of whatever colour, I hated its beauty and its magic and the secret I would never know. I hated its indifference and the cruelty which was part of its loveliness. Above all I hated her. For she belonged to the magic and the loveliness. She had left
35 me thirsty and all my life would be thirst and longing for what I had lost before I found it.

thirst in WSS = hunger in JE

So we rode away and left it – the hidden place. Not for me and not for her. I'd look after that. She's far along the road now.

Very soon she'll join all the others who know the secret and will not tell it. Or cannot. Or try and fail because they do not know enough. They can be recognized. White faces, dazed eyes, aimless gestures, high-pitched laughter. The way they walk and talk and scream or try to kill (themselves or you) if you laugh back at them. Yes, they've got to be watched. For the time comes when they try to kill, then disappear. But others are waiting to take their places, it's a long, long line. She's one of them. I too can wait – for the day when she is only a memory to be avoided, locked away, and like all memories a legend. Or a lie. . . .

I remember that as we turned the corner, I thought about Baptiste and wondered if he had another name – I'd never asked. And then that I'd sell the place for what it would fetch. I had meant to give it back to her. Now – what's the use?

That stupid boy followed us, the basket balanced on his head. He used the back of his hand to wipe away his tears. Who would have thought that any boy would cry like that. For nothing. Nothing. . . .

Part Three

'They knew that he was in Jamaica when his father and his brother died,' Grace Poole said. 'He inherited everything, but he was a wealthy man before that. Some people are fortunate, they said, and there were hints about the woman he brought back to England with him. Next day
5 Mrs Eff wanted to see me and she complained about gossip. I don't allow gossip. I told you that when you came. Servants will talk and you can't stop them, I said. And I am not certain that the situation will suit me, madam. First when I answered your advertisement you said that the person I had to look after was not a young girl. I asked if she was an old
10 woman and you said no. Now that I see her I don't know what to think. She sits shivering and she is so thin. If she dies on my hands who will get the blame? Wait, Grace, she said. She was holding a letter. Before you decide will you listen to what the master of the house has to say about this matter. "If Mrs Poole is satisfactory why not give her double, treble
15 the money," she read, and folded the letter away but not before I had seen the words on the next page, "but for God's sake let me hear no more of it." There was a foreign stamp on the envelope. "I don't serve the devil for no money," I said. She said, "If you imagine that when you serve this gentleman you are serving the devil you never made a greater
20 mistake in your life. I knew him as a boy. I knew him as a young man. He was gentle, generous, brave. His stay in the West Indies has changed him out of all knowledge. He has grey in his hair and misery in his eyes. Don't ask me to pity anyone who had a hand in that. I've said enough and too much. I am not prepared to treble your money, Grace, but I am
25 prepared to double it. But there must be no more gossip. If there is I will dismiss you at once. I do not think it will be impossible to fill your place. I'm sure you understand." Yes, I understand, I said.

protection? prison? both?

'Then all the servants were sent away and she engaged a cook, one maid and you, Leah. They were sent away but how could she stop them talking? If you ask me the whole county knows. The rumours I've heard – very far from the truth. But I don't contradict, I know better than to say a word. After all the house is big and safe, a shelter from the world outside which, say what you like, can be a black and cruel world to a woman. Maybe that's why I stayed on.' 5

The thick walls, she thought. Past the lodge gate a long avenue of trees and inside the house the blazing fires and the crimson and white rooms. But above all the thick walls, keeping away all the things that 10 you have fought till you can fight no more. Yes, maybe that's why we all stay Mrs Eff und Leah and me. All of us except that girl who lives in her own darkness. I'll say one thing for her, she hasn't lost her spirit. She's still fierce. I don't turn my back on her when her eyes have that look. I know it. 15

opening with Antoinette's voice

In this room I wake early and lie shivering for it is very cold. At last Grace Poole, the woman who looks after me, lights a fire with paper and sticks and lumps of coal. She kneels to blow it with bellows. The paper shrivels, the sticks crackle and spit, the coal smoulders and glowers. In the end flames shoot up and they are 20 beautiful. I get out of bed and go close to watch them and to wonder why I have been brought here. For what reason? There must be a reason. What is it that I must do? When I first came I thought it would be for a day, two days, a week perhaps. I thought that when I saw him and spoke to him I would be wise as serpents, 25 harmless as doves. 'I give you all I have freely,' I would say, 'and I will not trouble you again if you will let me go.' But he never came.

The woman Grace sleeps in my room. At night I sometimes see her sitting at the table counting money. She holds a gold piece in her hand and smiles. Then she puts it all into a little canvas bag 30 with a drawstring and hangs the bag round her neck so that it is hidden in her dress. At first she used to look at me before she did this but I always pretended to be asleep, now she does not trouble about me. She drinks from a bottle on the table then she goes to bed, or puts her arms on the table, her head on her arms, and 35

Antoinette's fate is controlled by Charlotte Bronte

sleeps. But I lie watching the fire die out. When she is snoring I get up and I have tasted the drink without colour in the bottle. The first time I did this I wanted to spit it out but managed to swallow it. When I got back into bed I could remember more and think again. I was not so cold.

lost touch with the outside world.

→ moving towards understanding ironically by drinking

There is one window high up – you cannot see out of it. My bed had doors but they have been taken away. There is not much else in the room. Her bed, a black press, the table in the middle and two black chairs carved with fruit and flowers. They have high backs and no arms. The dressing-room is very small, the room next to this one is hung with tapestry. Looking at the tapestry one day I recognized my mother dressed in an evening gown but with bare feet. She looked away from me, over my head just as she used to do. I wouldn't tell Grace this. Her name oughtn't to be Grace. Names matter, like when he wouldn't call me Antoinette, and I saw Antoinette drifting out of the window with her scents, her pretty clothes and her looking-glass. *all associated w identity*

There is no looking-glass here and I don't know what I am like now. I remember watching myself brush my hair and how my eyes looked back at me. The girl I saw was myself yet not quite myself. Long ago when I was a child and very lonely I tried to kiss her. But the glass was between us – hard, cold and misted over with my breath. Now they have taken everything away. What am I doing in this place and who am I?

The door of the tapestry room is kept locked. It leads, I know, into a passage. That is where Grace stands and talks to another woman whom I have never seen. Her name is Leah. I listen but I cannot understand what they say.

So there is still the sound of whispering that I have heard all my life, but these are different voices.

When night comes, and she has had several drinks and sleeps, it is easy to take the keys. I know now where she keeps them. Then I open the door and walk into their world. It is, as I always knew, made of cardboard. I have seen it before somewhere, this cardboard world where everything is coloured brown or dark red or yellow

that has <u>no light in it</u>. As I walk along the passages I wish I could
see what is behind the cardboard. They tell me I am in England
but I don't believe them. We lost our way to England. When?
Where? I don't remember, but we lost it. Was it that evening in the
cabin when he found me talking to the young man who brought   5
me my food? I put my arms round his neck and asked him to help
me. He said, 'I didn't know what to do, sir.' I smashed the glasses
and plates against the porthole. I hoped it would break and the sea
come in. A woman came and then an older man who cleared up
the broken things on the floor. He did not look at me while he was   10
doing it. The third man said drink this and you will sleep. I drank
it and I said, 'It isn't like it seems to be.' – 'I know. It never is,' he
said. And then I slept. When I woke it was a different sea. Colder.
It was that night, I think, that we changed course and lost our way
to England. This cardboard house where I walk at night is not   15
England.

One morning when I woke I ached all over. Not the cold, another
sort of ache. I saw that my wrists were red and swollen. Grace said,
'I suppose you're going to tell me that you don't remember anything
about last night.'   20

'When was last night?' I said.

'Yesterday.'

'I don't remember yesterday.'   *Mr. Mason gets stabbed*

'Last night a gentleman came to see you,' she said.

'Which of them was that?'   25

Because I knew that there were strange people in the house.
When I took the keys and went into the passage I heard them
laughing and talking in the distance, like birds, and there were
lights on the floor beneath.

Turning a corner I saw a girl coming out of her bedroom. She   30
wore a white dress and she was humming to herself. I flattened
myself against the wall for I did not wish her to see me, but she
stopped and looked round. She saw nothing but shadows, I took
care of that, but she didn't walk to the head of the stairs. She ran.
She met another girl and the second girl said, 'Have you seen a   35

ghost?' – 'I didn't see anything but I thought I felt something.' – 'That is the ghost,' the second one said and they went down the stairs together.

'Which of these people came to see me, Grace Poole?' I said.

5   He didn't come. Even if I was asleep I would have known. He hasn't come yet. She said, 'It's my belief that you remember much more than you pretend to remember. Why did you behave like that when I had promised you would be quiet and sensible? I'll never try and do you a good turn again. Your brother came to see

10 you.'

'I have no brother.'

'He said he was your brother.'

A long long way my mind reached back.

'Was his name Richard?'

15   'He didn't tell me what his name was.'

'I know him,' I said, and jumped out of bed. 'It's all here, it's all here, but I hid it from your beastly eyes as I hide everything. But where is it? Where did I hide it? The sole of my shoes? Underneath the mattress? On top of the press? In the pocket of my red dress?

20 Where, where is this letter? It was short because I remembered that Richard did not like long letters. Dear Richard please take me away from this place where I am dying because it is so cold and dark.'

Mrs Poole said, 'It's no use running around and looking now. He's gone and he won't come back – nor would I in his place.'

25   I said, 'I can't remember what happened. I can't remember.'

'When he came in,' said Grace Poole, 'he didn't recognize you.'

'Will you light the fire,' I said, 'because I'm so cold.'

'This gentleman arrived suddenly and insisted on seeing you and that was all the thanks he got. You rushed at him with a knife

30 and when he got the knife away you bit his arm. You won't see him again. And where did you get that knife? I told them you stole it from me but I'm much too careful. I'm used to your sort. You got no knife from me. You must have bought it that day when I took you out. I told Mrs Eff you ought to be taken out.'

35   'When we went to England,' I said.

'You fool,' she said, 'this is England.'

[handwritten note: answers the question of how Antoinette got the knife in Jane Eyre.]

'I don't believe it,' I said, 'and I never will believe it.'

(That afternoon we went to England. There was grass and olive-green water and tall trees looking into the water. This, I thought, is England. If I could be here I could be well again and the sound in my head would stop. Let me stay a little longer, I said, 5 and she sat down under a tree and went to sleep. A little way off there was a cart and horse – a woman was driving it. It was she who sold me the knife. I gave her the locket round my neck for it.) *[handwritten note: given to her by Aunt Cora]*

Grace Poole said, 'So you don't remember that you attacked this gentleman with a knife? I said that you would be quiet. "I must 10 speak to her," he said. Oh he was warned but he wouldn't listen. I was in the room but I didn't hear all he said except "I cannot interfere legally between yourself and your husband." It was when he said "legally" that you flew at him and when he twisted the knife out of your hand you bit him. Do you mean to say that you 15 don't remember any of this?'

I remember now that he did not recognize me. I saw him look at me and his eyes went first to one corner and then to another, not finding what they expected. He looked at me and spoke to me as though I were a stranger. What do you do when something happens 20 to you like that? Why are you laughing at me? 'Have you hidden my red dress too? If I'd been wearing that he'd have known me.'

'Nobody's hidden your dress,' she said. 'It's hanging in the press.' *[handwritten note: big symbol of Antoinette's identity]*

She looked at me and said, 'I don't believe you know how long 25 you've been here, you poor creature.'

'On the contrary,' I said, 'only I know how long I have been here. Nights and days and days and nights, hundreds of them slipping through my fingers. But that does not matter. Time has no meaning. But something you can touch and hold like my red 30 dress, that has a meaning. Where is it?' *[handwritten note: no sense of time or place]*

She jerked her head towards the press and the corners of her mouth turned down. As soon as I turned the key I saw it hanging, the colour of fire and sunset. The colour of flamboyant flowers. 'If you are buried under a flamboyant tree,' I said, 'your soul is lifted 35 up when it flowers. Everyone wants that.'

She shook her head but she did not move or touch me.

The scent that came from the dress was very faint at first, then it grew stronger. The smell of vetiver and frangipani, of cinnamon and dust and lime trees when they are flowering. The smell of the sun and the smell of the rain.

identity she got so strongly from her previous setting is retained in the one thing she brought.

...I was wearing a dress of that colour when Sandi came to see me for the last time.

shift to past memory

'Will you come with me?' he said. 'No,' I said, 'I cannot.'

'So this is good-bye?'

'Yes, this is good-bye.'

'But I can't leave you like this,' he said, 'you are unhappy.'

'You are wasting time,' I said, 'and we have so little.'

Sandi often came to see me when that man was away and when I went out driving I would meet him. I could go out driving then. The servants knew, but none of them told.

Now there was no time left so we kissed each other in that stupid room. Spread fans decorated the walls. We had often kissed before but not like that. That was the life and death kiss and you only know a long time afterwards what it is, the life and death kiss. The white ship whistled three times, once gaily, once calling, once to say good-bye. → *experiences another death because she is leaving*

I took the red dress down and put it against myself. 'Does it make me look intemperate and unchaste?' I said. That man told me so. He had found out that Sandi had been to the house and that I went to see him. I never knew who told. 'Infamous daughter of an infamous mother,' he said to me.

'Oh put it away,' Grace Poole said, 'come and eat your food. Here's your grey wrapper. Why they can't give you anything better is more than I can understand. They're rich enough.'

But I held the dress in my hand wondering if they had done the last and worst thing. If they had *changed* it when I wasn't looking. If they had changed it and it wasn't my dress at all – but how could they get the scent?

'Well don't stand there shivering,' she said, quite kindly for her.

I let the dress fall on the floor, and looked from the fire to the dress and from the dress to the fire. transforming identity

I put the grey wrapper round my shoulders, but I told her I wasn't hungry and she didn't try to force me to eat as she sometimes does.

'It's just as well that you don't remember last night,' she said. 'The gentleman fainted and a fine outcry there was up here. Blood all over the place and I was blamed for letting you attack him. And the master is expected in a few days. I'll never try to help you again. You are too far gone to be helped.'

I said, 'If I had been wearing my red dress Richard would have known me.'

'Your red dress,' she said, and laughed.

But I looked at the dress on the floor and it was as if the fire had spread across the room. It was beautiful and it reminded me of something I must do. I will remember I thought. I will remember quite soon now.

the lighting of fire / Thornfield burning is connected to her identity.

That was the third time I had my dream, and it ended. I know now that the flight of steps leads to this room where I lie watching the woman asleep with her head on her arms. In my dream I waited till she began to snore, then I got up, took the keys and let myself out with a candle in my hand. It was easier this time than ever before and I walked as though I were flying.

All the people who had been staying in the house had gone, for the bedroom doors were shut, but it seemed to me that someone was following me, someone was chasing me, laughing. Sometimes I looked to the right or to the left but I never looked behind me for I did not want to see that ghost of a woman whom they say haunts this place. I went down the staircase. I went further than I had ever been before. There was someone talking in one of the rooms. I passed it without noise, slowly.

At last I was in the hall where a lamp was burning. I remember that when I came. A lamp and the dark staircase and the veil over my face. They think I don't remember but I do. There was a door to the right. I opened it and went in. It was a large room with a red

5

10

15

20

25

30

35

no meaning

carpet and red curtains. Everything else was white I sat down on a couch to look at it and it seemed sad and cold and empty to me, like a church without an altar. I wished to see it clearly so I lit all the candles, and there were many. I lit them carefully from the one I was carrying but I couldn't reach up to the chandelier. Then I looked round for the altar for with so many candles and so much red, the room reminded me of a church. Then I heard a clock ticking and it was made of gold. Gold is the idol they worship.

Suddenly I felt very miserable in that room, though the couch I was sitting on was so soft that I sank into it. It seemed to me that I was going to sleep. Then I imagined that I heard a footstep and I thought what will they say, what will they do if they find me here? I held my right wrist with my left hand and waited. But it was nothing. I was very tired after this. Very tired. I wanted to get out of the room but my own candle had burned down and I took one of the others. Suddenly I was in Aunt Cora's room. I saw the sunlight coming through the window, the tree outside and the shadows of the leaves on the floor, but I saw the wax candles too and I hated them. So I knocked them all down. Most of them went out but one caught the thin curtains that were behind the red ones. I laughed when I saw the lovely colour spreading so fast, but I did not stay to watch it. I went into the hall again with the tall candle in my hand. It was then that I saw her — the ghost. The woman with streaming hair. She was surrounded by a gilt frame but I knew her. I dropped the candle I was carrying and it caught the end of a tablecloth and I saw flames shoot up. As I ran or perhaps floated or flew I called help me Christophine help me and looking behind me I saw that I had been helped. There was a wall of fire protecting me but it was too hot, it scorched me and I went away from it.

There were more candles on a table and I took one of them and ran up the first flight of stairs and the second. On the second floor I threw away the candle. But I did not stay to watch. I ran up the last flight of stairs and along the passage. I passed the room where they brought me yesterday or the day before yesterday, I don't remember. Perhaps it was quite long ago for I seemed to know

direct reference to gold
really the reasoning is there

Dream world almost becomes reality for Antoinette.

when she jumps, it is because she imagines she is jumping back into her old life, into her identity.

positive + negative in her jump   PARADOXICAL **Part Three**
▷ she dies because she is giving herself freedom

the house quite well. I knew how to get away from the heat and the shouting, for there was shouting now. When I was out on the battlements it was cool and I could hardly hear them. I sat there quietly. I don't know how long I sat. Then I turned round and saw the sky. It was red and all my life was in it. I saw the grandfather 5 clock and Aunt Cora's patchwork, all colours, I saw the orchids and the stephanotis and the jasmine and the tree of life in flames. I saw the chandelier and the red carpet downstairs and the bamboos and the tree ferns, the gold ferns and the silver, and the soft green velvet of the moss on the garden wall. I saw my doll's house and 10 the books and the picture of the Miller's Daughter. I heard the parrot call as he did when he saw a stranger, *Qui est là? Qui est là?* and the man who hated me was calling too, Bertha! Bertha! The wind caught my hair and it streamed out like wings. It might bear me up, I thought, if I jumped to those hard stones. But when I 15 looked over the edge I saw the pool at Coulibri. Tia was there. She beckoned to me and when I hesitated, she laughed. I heard her say, You frightened? And I heard the man's voice, Bertha! Bertha! All this I saw and heard in a fraction of a second. And the sky so red. Someone screamed and I thought, *Why did I scream?* I called 20 'Tia!' and jumped and woke. ⎰ dream ends.

Grace Poole was sitting at the table but she had heard the scream too, for she said, 'What was that?' She got up, came over and looked at me. I lay still, breathing evenly with my eyes shut. 'I must have been dreaming,' she said. Then she went back, not to the 25 table but to her bed. I waited a long time after I heard her snore, then I got up, took the keys and unlocked the door. I was outside holding my candle. Now at last I know why I was brought here and what I have to do. There must have been a draught for the flame flickered and I thought it was out. But I shielded it with my hand 30 and it burned up again to light me along the dark passage.

In the paragraph, Antoinette is calm, in control.
    FIRST PERSON
        ▷ she is doing everything for herself
        ▷ strength of "I"
        ▷ agency over her actions

Language Notes and Activities

PART ONE, PAGES 3–23

Focus

This part of the story is told by Antoinette, who describes her childhood on the Coulibri estate. She shows us how the place has decayed since the death of her father and the abolition of slavery, and then the changes that come with the remarriage of her mother to an Englishman. Past and present are very important, as are change, premonition and fear.

Think about how Jean Rhys describes Coulibri, and Antoinette's feelings about it. What kind of relationships does Antoinette have with her mother, brother, and the servants?

Whom does she feel closest to?

What impact does the arrival of Mr Mason have on the family?

How many dreams does she have and what are they about?

Follow-up

How would you describe the atmosphere of Coulibri?

Think about how Jean Rhys uses dresses, hair, mirrors and dreams to further the story.

Describe Antoinette's relationship with Tia: why does Antoinette say 'It was as if I saw myself' (p. 23.33)?

What things change when Mr Mason comes into their lives?

when trouble comes close ranks (3.1): people should group together to face difficulties. *ranks*: social or military groups.

we were not in their ranks (3.2): Antoinette's family are Creoles. They are white, though possibly with some distant black ancestors, and they have lived there for generations. They feel excluded by the rich white incomers and the wealthier plantation owners.

she pretty like pretty self (3.3): she is as pretty as prettiness itself is (an example of the English Creole language which Christophine speaks).

Martinique girl (3.6): She came from another island, colonized by the French rather than the English, and therefore regarded as different.

Spanish Town (3.8): the capital of Jamaica. The Spanish were the first colonizers.

Coulibri (3.8): the name of the estate where Antoinette lives. It means 'humming bird'.

thing of the past (3.9): it doesn't happen any more.

compensation (3.13): When slavery was abolished in 1833, slave-owners were promised money for each slave they set free.

Nelson's Rest (3.18): The French threatened to invade Jamaica at the end of the eighteenth century and again in 1806. The name of the estate identifies it with one of the British heroes who fought against Napoleon.

haunted (3.23): because the owner committed suicide.

looking-glass (3.26–7): mirror.

frangipani (4.6): a small tree with fragrant white, pale yellow or pink flowers.

marooned (4.10): isolated, cut off. The word originated in Jamaica, referring to the descendants of the slaves of the Spanish who fled to the mountains when the English invaded.

I too old (4.11): I am too old (another example of Creole language).

devil prince of this world (4.20): biblical quote from St John 12:31: 'Now is the judgment of this world; now shall the prince of this world be cast out.'

the tree of life (4.29): biblical reference to the garden of Eden in the book of Genesis, from which Adam and Eve were driven out because of their sins.

tree ferns (4.31): tropical ferns that grow as tall as trees.

glacis (5.7): a kind of veranda, running along the front of the house. From the French word *glacer*, to freeze.

patois (5.26): the French Creole of Martinique.

Adieu (5.31): adieu: farewell; *à dieu*: to God, in God's hands.

wedding present (6.18): She used to be a slave but is now free.

These new ones (6.34–5): incomers like Mason who don't understand the situation.

let sleeping curs lie (7.6): let sleeping dogs lie, meaning to leave well alone.

white cockroaches (7.20): household pests, associated with dirt, that are usually brown or black.

calabash (8.1): a large gourd used as a container.

Only talk (8.16): you only talk about it.

look like I drown dead (8.19): looked as if I had died by drowning.

salt fish (8.28): The slaves used to eat salt fish while their owners ate fresh.

flagstones (9.12): paving stones.

crazy in truth (9.29): really crazy.

Letter of the Law (10.8–9): They have set up a legal system; they *are* the law.

tread machine (10.10): Treadmills were powered by people treading on steps inside the wheel, and used for hard labour.

shamrock (10.36): Irish charm for good luck.

water wheel (11.10–11): Coulibri had been a sugar plantation, and the water wheel was used to crush the sugar cane.

smooth smiling people (11.26–7): Antoinette means that they are insincere.

fantastic marriage (11.30): a foolish marriage.

bastards (12.4): Antoinette's father had many illegitimate mixed-race children, to whom Annette and Antoinette behaved kindly.

pretty penny (12.6): a lot of money.

privy seat (12.9): lavatory seat.

idiot (12.12): Although Pierre is described as an idiot, the symptoms sound more like those of cystic fibrosis, which is not hereditary.

lowering expression (12.13): gloomy or sullen.

light as cotton (12.15–16): probably a reference to a song by Stephen Foster: 'I dream of Jeannie with the light brown hair / Borne as a vapour on the soft summer air.'

Trinidad (12.18): a British colony from 1802. Mason has estates there too, and in Antigua (14.19).

cheap (12.27): It was a good time to make a profit.

obeah (12.29): Christophine came from the French island of Martinique and was said to practise obeah or magic. The implication here is that she has brought Mason good luck, so far.

Providence (12.35): fate or destiny. Aunt Cora has not tried to make a profit from the situation like Mason. They do not trust each other.

None of you (13.9): Antoinette means the incomers like Mason.

They can smell money (13.12–13): The servants return now that they can be paid.

broken-down press (13.20): a broken cupboard.

dead man's dried hand (13.25–6): The sacrifice of a cock was common in obeah rituals, but the idea of the hand might have come from mixed traditions.

They invent stories . . . every day (14.20–21): The local people watch everything they do. Putting poison in food was part of obeah.

You don't like . . . the other side (14.27–8): Mason treats the local people as children. Annette treats them as equals.

the righteous (15.9): those whom God will save.

wedding (15.15): the local people don't marry. Mason assumes there is an innocent reason for the people not being at home as usual. In fact they are preparing to attack.

pappy (15.20): father.

glacis was not a good place (15.34): a warning about health, although the *glacis* is later dangerous for other reasons too.

coolies (16.21): workers from India were imported after 1833.

sect (17.2): religious group.

yellow roses (17.9): probably imported from England like 'The Miller's Daughter'.

Great mistake to go by looks (17.21): it is a big mistake to judge people by their appearance.

crib (17.25): a small child's bed.

shingle (18.6): a wooden tile from the roof.

tamarinds (19.6): the fruit of the tamarind tree used for medicine, food and drinks.

they get at the back (19.14): they have gone round to the back of the house.

Qui est là (21.6): Who is there?

Ché Coco (21.6–7): Dear Coco.

ladies' saddle (21.20): Women rode side-saddle in those days.

black Englishman (21.22): They are taunting Sass, the black servant.

flambeaux (21.29): flaming torches.

the ones who laughed (21.32): Antoinette is always afraid of people who laugh.

unlucky to kill a parrot (22.10–11): a superstition. Parrots were used in obeah.

cobblestone road (22.18–20): road paved with small stones.

machete (22.21): a large heavy knife used in the fields.

Myra she witness for us (22.26): Myra can verify that everything that happened was an accident.

You mash centipede . . . grow again (22.27–8): when you crush or cut up a centipede, but leave a small piece unharmed, it will grow again.

jumby (23.6): ghost, or person with magical powers. Probably from the West African word 'njamba', meaning 'spirit'.

sangoree (23.8): sangria, drink made from wine and fruit juice. From the Spanish 'a bleeding'.

PAGES 24–35

Focus

In this section we learn what has happened since the night of the fire: think about what has happened to Coulibri, to Pierre and to Annette.

Antoinette goes to school. What kind of people does she meet on the way to school, and who rescues her? How are the people she meets at school different from people she has met before? Which people are important to her?

Antoinette dreams again about Coulibri. Compare the two dreams.

Follow-up
Antoinette's life has changed completely. How does she feel about her new life in the convent?

There are many colours in this section. How many can you find? Compare Antoinette's embroidery on p. 29 with Aunt Cora's patchwork on p. 31. Why do you think these descriptions are here?

How does she feel when her stepfather comes to visit? What do you think might happen next?

But darker (24.8): Antoinette is suggesting that she knows she has negro blood.
arrowroot (24.12): a drink given to invalids.
hammock (24.19): a stretcher, a way of transporting people, especially over rough ground.
He died before that (24.26): She knew that Pierre's condition had been serious for a long time.
It's not her (25.29–30): She realizes that her mother has changed. She is then rejected by Annette for the second time.
convent (26.5): Antoinette is sent to a Roman Catholic convent school.
sandbox tree (26.9): a West Indian tree.
a white skin (26.11): The boy is an albino.
sans culottes (27.3): literally 'no trousers', but in the French Revolution it was a term for the extremists. Here it could refer to class or to mad behaviour.
zombie (27.4): one of the living dead, either one brought back to life or a living person whose spirit has been stolen by witchcraft.

Sandi (27.23): (Cosway) one of Antoinette's mixed-race cousins.

Oh la la (28.12): a French saying meaning 'Oh goodness me'.

Antoinette Mason (28.21): When her mother remarried Antoinette would have taken her stepfather's name.

1839 (29.20): six years after the Emancipation Act; Antoinette must be about fourteen. The only definite date in the novel.

The Relics (29.24): The implication is that the Saint's bones came from Europe, but Antoinette notes that she is not in the book, so the relics are unlikely to be genuine.

Here Theophilus (29.31–2): The saints, like the nuns, were married to Christ and the Church.

mine does not look like yours (30.21): The favoured girls are not mixed race.

cask (30.24): a barrel. Nuns are not supposed to look at themselves.

bar accidents (31.1): assuming nothing unfortunate happened.

vetiver (31.2): scent made from a grass plant.

whom I must forget (31.10): Annette has gone mad and been shut away.

patchwork counterpane (31.19): a bedspread made by hand, consisting of many small pieces of material sewn together.

chemises (32.2): long shirts or slips.

now and at the hour (32.6–7, 7–8): quotation from the Roman Catholic prayer Hail Mary.

Let perpetual light (32.8): from the Prayer for the Dead.

It is a different light (32.11): Antoinette thinks of her mother in the real light, as in the garden at Coulibri. As usual, she keeps her thoughts to herself.

gabble (32.14): to say the prayers quickly without thinking what they mean.

Everything was brightness, or dark (32.17): She refers both to the climate and to the religion.

I could not wear (33.2): because of the convent rules.

different (33.3): She senses that he is about to persuade her to do something that will please him. He mentions the man that might ask to marry her.

lax (33.23): not following the rules strictly.

Say nothing . . . be true (34.1–2): if I don't talk about it, then it might not happen.

dream (34.7): compare p. 10.

my mother's funeral (35.7): Her mother died the year before, and the words of the prayers she has learnt at school do not help.

the devil must have (35.19): from the saying 'The devil must have his day', meaning evil things happen. The nun thinks Antoinette is referring just to her mother's death, but she is thinking back to her mother living in poverty.

PART TWO, PAGES 36–56

Focus

Antoinette and the nameless Englishman (Mr Rochester) have married, and go to Granbois on the island of Dominica for their honeymoon. The estate used to belong to Antoinette's mother.

Mr Rochester is the narrator: how does he describe the place at the beginning of this section, and how do his feelings change (or stay the same)?

What are the differences between Antoinette and Mr Rochester?

What do we learn about how their marriage came about?

Why do you think he marries her? Why does she marry him?

She feels at home at Granbois, why doesn't he?

Think about how the author conveys the differences between night and day.

Compare their attitudes to the place, the servants, the scents, England.

During this section Mr Rochester begins to feel uncomfortable: what particular things make him feel uncomfortable?

Follow-up

How would you summarize the differences between Antoinette and Mr Rochester?

Do you think they can overcome these?

Granbois is a very female kind of place: what does Mr Rochester feel about it?

How would you describe their physical relationship?

Inside and outside, night and day, male and female, these are all important contrasts. Think about how Jean Rhys structures this section.

What are the main differences between the beginning and the end of this section?

for better or for worse (36.2): echo of the marriage service in the Church of England (ironic in this case).

mango (36.3): a tree with very sweet fruit.

half-caste (36.4): the word he uses for mixed race.

shingly (36.14): stony.

Massacre (36.16): a village near Jean Rhys's birthplace on Dominica. The local people deny the history behind the name, which seems to come from the fact that a mixed-race man was killed by his white half-brother.

Long, sad, dark alien eyes (37.21): He is implying that she has mixed blood.

Dear Father (37.33): Rochester's father arranged the marriage for his son, who feels uncomfortable about it.

Bon sirop (39.9): good syrup, a good drink.

extreme green (39.16): He is struck by the vibrant colours. Later he finds them menacing.

Granbois (39.19): the name of the estate means 'big woods'.

blue . . . purple . . . green (39.22): the colours Antoinette chose for her embroidery on p. 29.

No provision (39.27–8): This is ominous for Antoinette's future.

Her family have given her away to a stranger, and signed her money over to him, as was the law.

sold my soul (39.32): reference to the Faust legend. Faust sold his soul to the devil in exchange for knowledge, power and wealth during his lifetime.

And yet . . . (39.33–4): Hers is not an English beauty. He is thinking about race.

da (41.11): Creole for nurse.

Doudou, ché cocotte (41.22): dear little chicken.

rum punch (42.4): a local drink. Rum is made from sugar cane.

wreaths (42.11): Here the wreaths are to celebrate their marriage, but in England wreaths are used at funerals.

dressed up to the nines (42.31–2): dressed up in their finery.

Byron . . . Eater (43.19–20): books popular in the 1820s.

drawer (44.8): He never posts his letter and he says that his thoughts will never be known.

I played the part (44.13–14): He is describing how they met. The marriage had been arranged by Rochester's father and Antoinette's stepfather. After his death, Richard Mason, Antoinette's stepbrother, took over responsibility for it.

All benevolent. All slave-owners (44.22): highly ironic.

the way you laughed (45.36): Antoinette is fearful, but he persuades her by promising her peace, happiness and safety, but not love.

à la Joséphine (46.26–7): after Empress Josephine. They follow French fashions, but are rather out of date.

Coralita (46.31): coral-coloured flowers.

crumb brush (47.1–2): small brush for sweeping the tablecloth.

England is like a dream? (47.3): Antoinette has never been there, so it is a reasonable question. He replies angrily that her world seems like a dream to him, even though he is in it.

scent (47.18): He dislikes strong scents. He can ask Antoinette not to put them on her hair (p. 46) but he can't control the flowers. The scents are stronger at night.

Crac-cracs (47.20): insects like crickets.

La belle (47.24): the beauty.

moonlight (48.35): In many cultures the moon is associated with madness.

cassava . . . jelly (50.1–2): a fleshy root that can be made into flour. Guava is a kind of fruit.

bull's blood (50.12): coffee.

Rose elle a vécu (51.10): from a poem written in 1599 by François de Malherbe as an elegy for a dead girl. 'Rose has lived as roses live, for one morning.'

that is not nothing (52.8): it is hiding something.

fer de lance (52.17): a large, poisonous snake.

Sandi (52.31): Sandi Cosway, her cousin.

More than a person (53.15): I love this place more than I love people.

if she asked no questions (54.1–2): She trusts the servants, he does not.

whims and fancies (54.12): He interprets local custom as Christophine's power.

Adieu foulard (55.5): quotation from a song, 'goodbye foulard [silk or a mixture of silk and cotton], goodbye madras [cotton or a mixture of silk and cotton]'.

Ma belle (55.5): In the song the girl asks her mother why beautiful flowers die in a day.

die (55.31): sexual orgasm.

a stranger (56.15): He cannot consider her an equal.

Her mind was already made up (56.34): She is keen to learn more about England in order to get nearer to him, but he sees her lack of knowledge as her inability to understand.

PAGES 57–66

Focus

In this section something critical happens. All Rochester's unease is confirmed by the letter he receives. Why do you think he believes everything in the letter?

What is the immediate effect on his relationship with Antoinette?

Why does Christophine decide to leave?

What is the meaning of Amélie's song?

Rochester reacts by going for a walk. Think about how he describes the forest. What does he find there?

Follow-up

What has changed in the relationship between Antoinette and Rochester?

How far do you accept what Daniel Cosway says in his letter?

How have Rochester's descriptions of the forest changed?

There are many references to magic in this section. How do they add to our understanding of how Rochester feels about the place?

copperplate (57.22): old-fashioned handwriting.

hermit (57.24): someone who lives an isolated life by choice.

madness (58.6): He implies that the whole family is mad, although he excludes himself.

don't like me (58.13–14): didn't like me.

reprobate (58.17): Antoinette's father.

hide herself (58.32): He implies that even Antoinette's shyness is a sign of madness.

kill her husband (59.3–4): as Bertha Mason tries to do in *Jane Eyre*.

cypher (59.30): work things out.

nancy stories (60.10): local stories about Anansi (also known as Anancy, Anance, Ananse), the clever spider of Ashanti and Caribbean folk tales.

obt (60.20): obedient.

look like he see zombi (61.11): looks as if he has seen a ghost.

spunks (62.8): courage.

plantain (62.22): a type of banana used as a vegetable.

They all knew (63.33): He thinks everyone knew his wife was mad.

paved road (64.13): that is, people used to live and work in what is now a deserted place.

bunches of flowers (64.20): gifts to spirits as protection against magic.

screamed (64.25): She thinks he is a ghost.

pavé (65.12): paved.

'Obeah' (66.7): He is reading a book written by an Englishman, whose views confirm his own. Idea of poison again.

PAGES 66–74

Focus

This short section is spoken by Antoinette. What do we learn about her feelings for Christophine? For Rochester?

What does she think about England? Does she want to go there?

What does she mean about the bed with the red curtains?

Follow-up

Why do you think the author puts this part back into Antoinette's voice?

Why does she want to use obeah? What does Christophine think? Do you think it will work?

How do you feel about Antoinette's situation?

I (66.21): The narrative returns to Antoinette.

hibiscus (67.25): pretty, flowering bush.

English law (68.19): This is the first time Christophine understands the situation. She thinks it sounds too unjust to be lawful.

Ask him pretty (68.23): ask him nicely.

rosy pink (69.2): The British Empire used to be coloured pink in school atlases.

red curtains (69.13): refers to the bed in *Jane Eyre*.

tim-tim story (70.11): fairy story.

béké (70.13): a white person.

doudou (70.20): sweetheart.

Bertha . . . mother's name (70.26–8): Her mother's name was Annette.

It's disgraceful (71.21): like Christophine, Aunt Cora was horrified by the lack of care taken by her male relatives to protect Antoinette.

lines and circles (72.30): She thinks this must be to do with magic.

soucriant (73.2): a wailing ghost. Antoinette is beginning to look like a zombie.

chicken feathers (73.22): used in the magic ceremonies.

Nearby . . . what he did? (74.4–7): in the Bible, Judas betrays Christ for money. (Peter also rejects Jesus, and the cock crow is the symbol of his betrayal).

It was wrapped in a leaf (74.13–14): Christophine gives Antoinette some magic powder to use to get back her husband's love on the understanding that she will try to talk to him first.

PAGES 74–106

Focus

In this section we return to Rochester's narrative. What is the effect of this?

He receives a second letter from Daniel Cosway. Think about what Amélie tells him about Daniel. What is her attitude to Daniel and to Rochester? What does she imply about Antoinette? Why does Amélie later betray her?

Rochester goes to see Daniel, who gives him more information about Antoinette and her family. Do you believe him? Does Rochester?

Think about how Rochester's attitude towards Antoinette changes during this section. There are a number of turning points: which would you say was the most significant?

Language Notes and Activities

Follow-up

What was the effect of Christophine's magic potion? Was it what Antoinette wanted?

Christophine knew that it might not work, so why do you think she gave in to Antoinette? Do you think the potion made the situation worse?

How does Rochester's relationship with Amélie parallel his with Antoinette?

What is the effect of his betrayal on Antoinette?

This is the first time Rochester has spoken to Christophine about Antoinette. Whose view do you sympathize with most?

Rochester blames his father for the situation he is in. Do you think he is as much a victim of circumstance as Antoinette?

coloured (76.1): mixed race.

Mr Sandi get married (76.12): Sandi Cosway, her cousin. 'Get married' might mean 'have a sexual relationship'.

Vengeance is Mine (76.31): biblical quotation.

They call me Daniel . . . Esau (77.1–2): Daniel and Esau are biblical characters. Esau was the elder of twin sons, who sold his birthright to his brother Jacob for a bowl of food. He is considered a bad brother. Daniel survived the lions' den because of his faith.

tablet (77.3): commemorative stone or gravestone on the wall of the church.

stone (77.6): see above.

Pious . . . Beloved by all (77.7): quotations from the tablet.

people he buy (77.8): slaves.

five six (77.22): five or six.

sly-boots (77.33): a cunning or crafty person.

two-faced (78.26): insincere.

go to jail (78.28): He implies that she was sent to jail for practising magic.

no woman (79.5): any woman.

She start with Sandi (79.16): He implies that Sandi was Antoinette's first lover.

holding her left wrist (80.22): Perhaps the action reminds him of the shackles the slaves wore round their wrists and ankles.

two deaths (81.12): Antoinette said this about her brother too (p. 24).

quickly (81.17): one of the few suggestions that Antoinette might not always tell the truth.

the other side (81.20): Daniel knows you will believe him rather than me.

it is something else (82.21): the place does not belong to anyone, and cannot be controlled.

glass (83.3): mirror.

lies (83.26): She is referring to the stories told by Daniel Cosway.

ornamented iron (84.3): He corrects her, and she accepts the term 'wrought iron' instead.

Drink it (85.27): The implication is that her mother is being given alcohol to keep her helpless.

white powder (87.16): from Christophine.

She need not have done (87.28–9): i.e. use the magic potion. He implies he would have made love to her that night anyway.

poisoned (88.11): the after-effects of the potion.

thick eyebrows (88.25): He notices what he thinks are negroid facial characteristics (Antoinette said the same of her mother, p. 5).

thin partition (89.35): He does not care if his wife can hear them or not.

darker (90.2): He is looking for negroid characteristics.

Mr Fraser (91.28): the magistrate in Spanish Town.

get off lightly (92.15): There were strict laws against the practice of obeah.

Que komesse (94.3): Creole for 'what's wrong?'.

you do the same thing (94.22–3): you behave just as badly (i.e. by sleeping with the servants). But she also refers to how he is treating her.

justice (94.27): another example of how Rhys questions the meaning of words. Antoinette often says that there are two sides to everything.

Like you kissed mine (94.34): referring to p. 87.5.

That's obeah too (95.6): Calling someone by a different name was thought to be like putting on a curse.

Grandpappy (95.26): grandfather. He was a supporter of the Jacobite claim to the throne of England. James II went into exile in France in 1688, and his supporters would drink to the king 'over the water'.

Benky (95.31): crooked. Bonnie Prince Charlie was the son of James II, who claimed the throne (unsuccessfully) in 1745.

nightmare (96.12): This echoes scenes in *Jane Eyre*.

green menace (96.26): He finds the greenness of his surroundings a threat.

'Ma belle ka di' (96.31): quotation from song (see note to p. 55.5).

Like a doll . . . marionette (96.35–6): He talks about her as if she were a puppet.

Ti moun . . . Doudou ché . . . do l'enfant do (96.36–97.2): little one . . . dear darling . . . sleep, child, sleep.

you pay for it one day (97.30): you will suffer one day for what you have done (she refers to his injuries from the fire at the end of *Jane Eyre*).

Prince Rupert . . . the Rine (98.20): one of Charles I's soldiers in the English Civil War in the seventeenth century. Another reference to English history that makes no sense in the Caribbean.

(Not the way you mean) (99.8): The phrases in brackets represent Rochester's thoughts, except 100.10–12 which seem to represent what Antoinette said to Christophine.

drive her to it (102.16): drove her mad by the way they treated her after the death of Pierre.

Give my sister (102.32): echo of what Antoinette's stepbrother, Richard Mason, said to Rochester when they married.

she won't be satisfy (102.34): It is Antoinette who won't be satisfied.

She don't come . . . her to marry (102.35–103.2): she didn't go to your house in England . . . you begged her to marry you.

You do that . . . Satan self (104.29–30): if you do that for money you are as wicked as the devil.

I would give my eyes (104.32): Rochester is blinded in the fire at the end of *Jane Eyre*.

Other things I know (105.14): She is illiterate but she says she has other powers, maybe magic.

the letter (105.19): to his father, blaming him for the failure of his marriage.

certain that you know (105.31): He assumes that his wife is mad and that his father knew about her condition before the marriage.

commodious (106.3): large.

liberally (106.5): generously, so long as they don't talk.

cock crowed (106.9): another echo of the biblical story about Peter's betrayal of Christ.

le bon Dieu (106.17): the good Lord, a quotation from a Creole song.

dormi (106.21): asleep. He now uses Creole words himself.

house (106.29): He anticipates Thornfield, his house in *Jane Eyre*, with his wife locked up in a room on the third floor.

PAGES 107–13

Focus

In this short section Antoinette and Rochester prepare to leave the West Indies for England. What do you think might happen? Can they be happy?

Rochester's style is extremely disjointed and confused. Is he mad?

He talks about having lost something; what has he lost? Is it his fault that he has lost it?

Follow-up

The last word of Part Two is 'Nothing', while the opening phrase is 'So it was all over'. What has happened in this part of the novel? Could things have been different?

It could be argued that every character has suffered. Who do you feel the most sympathy for?

oleanders (107.1): an evergreen, poisonous shrub with red or white flowers.

hurricane months (107.5): that time of the year when strong winds blow (he is also anticipating difficult times ahead for himself).

Pity . . . the blast (107.16): from Shakespeare's *Macbeth* I.vii.21.

She love you (107.23): He remembers what Christophine told him, but he decides it is the voice of the devil trying to tempt him, rather than the truth. From this point on, his narrative becomes increasingly distorted and cruel. It makes us wonder who is mad, Antoinette or Rochester?

babe (108.11): refers back to 107.16, and the idea of pity.

Morne (109.1): In this case she does not accept the English word.

Jack Spaniards (109.2): the first colonizers.

The Emerald Drop (109.3): a green flash or line sometimes seen at sunset. She thinks it brings good luck, but he associates green with evil.

everything I had imagined . . . false (109.31): He is totally confused about what has happened and what to believe. His thoughts and emotions swing backwards and forwards throughout this section.

Antoinetta (110.3): He now calls her Antoinetta (in *Jane Eyre*, p. 328, her name is given as Bertha Antoinetta Mason, daughter of Antoinetta). See also the play on names, 100.2.

solitaire (110.12): a kind of song thrush.

Marie Galante (110.19): an island named after the ship Columbus was in when he first saw it.

earthquake (110.22): There was an earthquake in 1692 which destroyed Port Royal, the old capital of Jamaica. These must all be stories Antoinette has told him from Caribbean history.

the law of treasure (110.27): The law of treasure trove is that if treasure is found, it must be handed over to the authorities, who will keep most of it.

questions which are not answered (110.30): rather as he himself found a fortune by marrying Antoinette, but could not find answers to all his questions.

paltry money (111.15): not true. Her fortune was £30,000, a great deal of money at the time.

That girl she look you . . . (111.16–17): He remembers what Daniel Cosway said (79.17).

ghost (111.25): He describes her as a zombie.

nameless boy (111.30): a boy servant who wishes to go with Rochester.

Magdalene (112.25): biblical reference to Mary Magdalene who wept profusely when Christ died.

all my life . . . (112.35): He implies that he knows he has destroyed something that he might have found precious, i.e. his wife's love. He goes on to compare her to a zombie, or a mad person, that might try to kill him, and says he must lock her away like a bad memory.

PART THREE PAGES 114–23

Focus
In this final section Antoinette takes up the narrative again, after a brief introduction by Grace Poole who is her jailer. She is now a prisoner at Thornfield Hall in England. Do you think she is mad? What is the evidence?

How would you describe Grace Poole's attitude to her?

Why does the red dress mean so much to Antoinette?

What kind of things does she remember from her childhood?

Follow-up
What do you think happens at the end?

Why does she like the colour red so much? What does it mean to her?

Think about the three dreams. Are they all the same dream? How does the author use these to structure the novel?

There are many references to ghosts through the novel. What do they add to the atmosphere?

Grace Poole (114.2): Antoinette's jailer at Thornfield Hall. The narrative is now set in England, and is closely linked to *Jane Eyre*. The section in italics is in Grace Poole's voice.

He inherited (114.2): Rochester's father and elder brother have died, so he has inherited the family wealth (and by implication there was no need for him to have married for money).

Mrs Eff (114.5): Mrs Fairfax, Rochester's housekeeper.

I don't serve the devil for no money (114.17): I am not going to do wrong, however much money I get.

pity anyone (114.23): by implication she blames Antoinette.

to a woman (115.6–7): She is referring to herself, but her comment applies also to Antoinette, and indeed to Jane Eyre.

I (115.16): The narration returns to Antoinette.

What is it that I must do? (115.23): She answers her question in the last paragraph of the novel.

wise as serpents (115.25): biblical reference.

drink (116.2): gin (cf. *Jane Eyre*, p. 483).

doors (116.7): Traditional box beds were built into the walls and had wooden doors. These have been removed so she can be observed.

tapestry (116.11): Rich people hung tapestries on their walls before the days of wallpaper. The tapestries often described mythical scenes.

Names matter (116.15): She feels that she lost her sense of self when he started to call her Bertha. She interprets this as the effect of magic.

looking-glass (116.17): Mirrors have been important all through the novel. Now, as in the convent, she does not have one.

whispering (116.29): She has always been lonely, surrounded by servants who spoke to each other rather than to her.

cardboard (116.34): It is as if she is walking into the world between the covers of *Jane Eyre*.

wrists were red (117.18): The novel intersects with *Jane Eyre* (for example p. 332, where Bertha has to be tied up in order to restrain her). Slaves too were tied by the wrists.

no brother (118.11): She is right in that he is only a stepbrother.

That afternoon (119.2): possibly when Grace Poole took her out. She felt sorry for her.

flamboyant flowers (119.34): red flowers of the flame tree. Red was always her favourite colour. She refers to a myth that says the tree brings good luck.

scent (120.2): The dress brings back memories of all the scents of her childhood.

Sandi (120.6): her cousin. In this paragraph she implies that they loved each other, and that they saw each other until the time Rochester took her away.

fire (121.1): anticipation of the fire.

my dream (121.18): see also p. 10 and p. 34.

steps (121.19): the steps at Coulibri that led to the garden.

ghost (121.28): She may be referring to Jane Eyre or to herself.

red (121.35): link to the Red Room at the beginning of *Jane Eyre* where the heroine is locked up.

held my right wrist (122.13): Rochester called this her annoying habit (p. 80.22) when she held her left wrist with her right hand. Perhaps this time she is looking in a mirror.

lovely colour (122.21): the flames.

ghost (122.23): herself in the mirror.

last flight (122.34): She is kept on the third floor (as in Rochester's drawing on p. 106), and see p. 331 in *Jane Eyre*.

battlements (123.3): low wall at the edge of the roof.

It was red (123.5): with fire.

tree of life (123.7): see also pp. 4.29, 10.26.

Tia (123.16): her childhood friend who later threw a stone at her.

man's voice (123.18): Rochester is trying to rescue her, as in *Jane Eyre*. He is also the man who followed her in her dream.

Grace Poole (123.22): it now looks as if it has all been a dream. She sets off down the corridor with her candle. We assume that she will set fire to the house (as in her dream and in *Jane Eyre*), but the ending is left ambiguous.

Further Activities and Study Questions

1. When you read *Wide Sargasso Sea*, think first of all about what it means to you: which bits do you enjoy, what kind of emotions does it evoke for you, what does it make you think about?

2. Then, if you have read *Jane Eyre*, compare the two stories, particularly the parts about Bertha Mason, and see how your understanding of *Jane Eyre* changes after reading Jean Rhys's novel. Think about the lives of the two heroines, Jane and Antoinette/ Bertha. Why do you think their lives are so different?

3. Jean Rhys thought of several different titles for her novel before settling on *Wide Sargasso Sea*. Do you think this was the best choice? What does the image add to our understanding of the novel?

4. Compare the early version of a passage from *Wide Sargasso Sea* below (published in *Art and Literature*, 1964, pp. 178–9) of the text with that in the final published version (*WSS*, pp. 4–5). What differences can you see between the style of the two versions and which do you prefer?

Our garden was large – the largest and most beautiful in the world I thought – it was that garden in the Bible, and the tree of life grew there. But it had gone wild. Long grass grew between the flagstones, and a smell of dead flowers mixed with the living fresh smell. The tree ferns were as tall as forest tree ferns and underneath them the light was green. Some of our orchids withered but others flourished, greedy looking, snaky looking or too beautiful, not to be touched. One in particular was exactly like an octopus – its thin long brown tentacles, bare of leaves, hung from a twisted root. Twice a year it flowered – then the scent was sweeter and stronger than anything else in the garden. Not an inch of tentacle showed – it was a bell-shaped mass of white and mauve and deep purple, wonderful to see. But I never wanted to go near it.

5. Jean Rhys uses a number of unreliable narrators in this novel. Is there anyone we can trust completely?

6. It has been said that all the characters are flawed in some way. Do you agree?

7. Discuss how much the author uses the following: colour; dress; mirrors; nature.

8. The novel is structured around binaries. Choose one and think about how it works: England / the West Indies; man / woman; reason / emotion; happiness / unhappiness; hope / despair; freedom / captivity.

9. 'Ghosts are everywhere in her work – the imprint of the past and all we have as memories. (*Jean Rhys Revisited*, p. 261). Do you agree?

10. One of the novel's themes is madness. How would you describe it? Was Annette mad? Was Antoinette mad? Were they driven mad? Was Rochester mad? How does Jean Rhys question conventional ideas of madness?

11. What is Jean Rhys's attitude to slavery? Does slavery corrupt?

12. Is *Wide Sargasso Sea* a Gothic novel in your opinion?

13. Does Jean Rhys use the natural world as a metaphor for human relationships? In your opinion does the natural environment play a role in forming our characters? Why does Antoinette love the wild and beautiful landscape that Rochester finds alien?

14. '*Wide Sargasso Sea* has been acknowledged as a ground-breaking analysis of the imperialism at the heart of British

culture' (*Jean Rhys*, p. 20). Do you agree with this? Is it a post-colonial novel?

15. How far can it be regarded as a feminist novel? Jill Neville for example compares Jean Rhys with Colette, observing that 'Colette who also studies Bohemia makes her impoverished females fight back and often win. Jean Rhys women have only their ability to perceive, note, mark and inwardly digest. A dangerous and unpopular habit' (Jill Neville reviewing *Sleep It Off Lady*, quoted by Lykiard, p. 102). Do you think this is true with regard to *Wide Sargasso Sea*?

16. Jean Rhys said she had a 'passion for stating the case of the underdog'; how far is this an accurate comment on Jean Rhys's description of society in this novel?

17. If modernism can be described as 'above all a self-conscious movement, a literary movement acutely aware of other writers' (*Jean Rhys*, p. 7), do you think it is useful to discuss *Wide Sargasso Sea* as a modernist or postmodernist novel?

Setting and Background Notes

The Caribbean Islands

The islands of the Caribbean, with their indigenous Carib and Arawak populations, were taken over first by the Spanish and then by the English and French with their African slaves. Each island developed differently, depending on the language, religion, history and culture of the colonizers. The islands referred to in *Wide Sargasso Sea* are Jamaica and Dominica, one of the Windward Islands. Rhys never visited Jamaica herself, and she often conflates the two. Coulibri, the estate where Antoinette grows up, is set on Jamaica, where the servants are Protestants and disapprove of Annette Cosway, who is from Martinique, a French colony, as is her servant Christophine. Christophine is Catholic, and speaks and dresses differently from the other servants. The European rivalry between the English and French was paralleled in the Caribbean. As Daniel Cosway says (p. 58), 'French and English like cat and dog in these islands since long time'.

The honeymoon island, in Part Two, is Dominica. There is a place called Massacre there and, although not explained in the novel, it probably got its name from the murder of a mixed-race man Indian Warner (English father and Carib mother) by his half-brother. The suspicion and fear of mixed blood runs through the book. The black and white populations mistrust each other because of the history of slavery. There is also a large mixed-race population, and few of the white families are racially unmixed. Antoinette's father has had many mixed-race children. The isolation experienced by Antoinette and her family probably reflects that of Jean Rhys's own family. When Jean Rhys was born, the population of Dominica was 30,000, of which approximately only 300 were whites.

Other islands referred to are Barbados, where Richard Mason went to school, the only island colonized exclusively by the British, while Baptiste comes from St Kitts, which was colonized by both the British and the French.

The History of Slavery

The Emancipation Act was passed in 1833, giving slave-owners until 1838 to free their slaves. They were offered £19 per slave (the market rate being £35). In addition to the loss of free labour on the plantations, the price of sugar fell by half with the introduction of free trade. The planters felt betrayed by the British government that had previously encouraged them. At the beginning of the book Rhys describes the decay of the estate at Coulibri, and the despair of planters like Luttrell, who commits suicide; and she shows how disadvantaged the planters were compared with incomers like Mason. She adjusts the dates of *Jane Eyre*, in order to set her story at this particular time in the history of the Caribbean.

She also mentions the fact that life did not necessarily improve for the black workers after 1833. Christophine refers to the new methods of exploiting the workers, and the great wealth that the less scrupulous incomers could make. Ironically, it is the wealth of Antoinette Cosway after her mother's death that makes her vulnerable to the fortune-hunter Mr Rochester.

Creole

The word Creole can be a noun or an adjective, and is generally used to describe indigenous peoples or languages. Jean Rhys describes Antoinette's family as white Creole because they have lived in the Caribbean for generations. However, a Creole language is one that has developed from a pidgin, or restricted, language, in this case from the English spoken by the slaves when they arrived in the Caribbean in order to communicate with their owners and each other. Rhys uses elements of Creole to convey the language the servants speak. She uses some Creole vocabulary, such as obeah (see below), and some grammatical characteristics, for example the omission of the verb 'to be', the use of adjectives as nouns ('she pretty like pretty self'), and the use of verbs without agreement. She shows that Creole can have a vitality and impact that standard English lacks.

Obeah

It was thought that obeah practitioners could cast spells and use witchcraft against their victims and, above all, that they could change them into zombies, or the living dead. In *Wide Sargasso Sea* Christophine has the status of healer and witch (partly because she comes from a different island and therefore looks and sounds different). Antoinette describes going into Christophine's room and thinking there might be a dead man's hand behind the cupboard. Later she goes to her to ask for magic help in her marriage.

Fear of being poisoned pervades the novel from the poisoned horse on the first page. The house servants are under suspicion because they prepare food; they are dangerous – in *Wide Sargasso Sea* they set fire to the house. Antoinette thinks her husband's power over her is obeah, and she accuses him of using obeah when he starts calling her by another name. Christophine thinks he has turned Antoinette into a zombie, and he describes Antoinette as 'only a ghost. A ghost in the grey daylight' (p. 111).

Character Notes

The three main characters are Antoinette, Rochester and Christophine, and the changing relationships between the three of them determine the action of the novel.

Antoinette Mason (née Cosway)

Antoinette's name is very similar to Annette, her mother's name, which may be a suggestion that their fates are linked, and that the daughter will not be able to escape the same fate as her mother. At the beginning of the novel Annette is lively and about to attract a second husband, whereas Antoinette is a quiet, observant child. She remains quite childlike throughout the novel, responding emotionally to places and people, and turning to her old nurse, Christophine, in moments of crisis.

Antoinette has fiercely loyal feelings for people and for the landscape of her home: 'I love it more than anywhere in the world. As if it were a person. More than a person,' (p. 53) she tells Rochester. She feels a similar passion for Rochester after their marriage, as Christophine tells him, 'She love you so much. She thirsty for you' (p. 102).

She is, however, rejected by all the people she allows herself to love, except Christophine. She is rejected twice by her mother, first when Annette realizes that Pierre's condition is incurable, and then again when Pierre dies. Despite this, she still loves her mother. She is also rejected by her only childhood friend, Tia, who steals her dress and later throws a stone at her face. Finally she is rejected by Rochester. She learns to love him, but he allows himself to be persuaded by lies and half-truths, and finally he abuses her by making love to Amélie in the room next to hers.

Antoinette is affectionate and generous. Rochester criticizes her for giving away money 'carelessly, not counting it' (p. 53), and giving food and drink to all visitors. Even at the very end of Part Two she tries to explain to Rochester why the boy is crying and to take him with them. She is also proud and courageous: she keeps many things to herself rather than tell people how she feels, and she tries to fight Rochester. At the end of the novel she escapes in her own way from the captivity he has put her in.

Mr Rochester

Rochester is never mentioned by name in this novel, but his character is developed through his own words in Part Two, and through those of Antoinette and Christophine in particular. Because he is nameless, the reader feels more distanced from him. He comes to the West Indies specifically to marry an heiress and make money; he is the younger son and his father has decided to give his fortune to his elder son (as was the tradition).

He is disorientated by arriving in a new country and by the speed with which the arrangements for his marriage are made. When Antoinette tries to call off the marriage, he insists on its going ahead because he can't face being jilted and returning home empty-handed. His feelings for both Antoinette and the West Indies go through a series of changes. To begin with, he is indifferent, then he begins to be infatuated by both his wife and the place. But he is still unsure of his feelings, and Daniel Cosway plays on his insecurity. He starts to think that Antoinette, and everyone else, has lied to him and trapped him. He then starts to hate his wife and the place, and makes love to Amélie to hurt both her and Antoinette. Despite his cruelty, he does realize that in destroying Antoinette he is also destroying himself and his own chance of happiness.

Christophine

Christophine is the only person whom Antoinette trusts throughout the book. She was a slave who was given as a wedding present to Annette by her husband, and she remained loyal even after she was set free. Annette recognizes that she would not have survived after her husband's death without Christophine's help, and both she and her daughter are grateful. We hear that the other servants only stay because of her.

Christophine loves Antoinette and is more of a mother to her than Annette can be. In her childhood she finds a friend for her, sings her songs, and gives her advice. Later she tries to protect her against Rochester.

Christophine is a strong woman who has never married herself. She says, 'I thank my God. I keep my money. I don't give it to no worthless man' (p. 68). She is feared by the other servants because she comes from a different island and dresses and speaks differently. She is also thought to practise obeah, but she is realistic. When Antoinette goes to ask for a love potion to make Rochester love her again, Christophine knows it won't work, yet she tries to help Antoinette. She advises her to leave Rochester, but she is horrified to hear that Rochester has been given all her money in the marriage settlement.

Annette and Pierre

Annette married very young, and is left in poverty when her husband dies. Her son Pierre is brain damaged (possibly he suffers from cystic fibrosis), and when she realizes that he will never grow up healthy she withdraws from her daughter, Antoinette. Later she marries an Englishman, Mr Mason, who finds her extremely attractive. She hopes that he will be able to help Pierre, but increasingly she disagrees with her husband's attitudes to the local people. She feels that he doesn't understand them, treating them like children. When violence finally breaks out, she risks her life to save Pierre's, but he dies soon afterwards. It is not clear what happens next, but Mr Mason has her shut away when she turns violent and attacks him. She is guarded by servants who treat her badly, and she finally dies when Antoinette is about sixteen, possibly by suicide. Antoinette is never clear about what happened.

Daniel Cosway

Daniel claims to be Antoinette's illegitimate half-brother, but whether he is or not is not clear. He contacts Rochester soon after the wedding and tells him half-truths that Rochester cannot resist. For example, Daniel claims that both Annette and Pierre were mad, and that Antoinette is showing the same signs. He also suggests that Antoinette has had lovers before, one being Sandi Cosway, and that Rochester has been tricked into making an unwise marriage. Rochester refuses to feel sorry for him or pay him the money he asks for, but he cannot resist the implications of what Daniel tells him.

Tia

Christophine finds a friend for Antoinette called Tia. For a while they play happily together, but then they quarrel and Tia steals her money and her dress. Later, on the night of the fire, Tia throws a stone at Antoinette. Rhys makes it clear that both children are the products of their society.

Mr Mason and the Luttrells

Mr Mason and his English friends, the Luttrells, have come to the West Indies to make money. The old Creole families like the Cosways have fallen into poverty after the Emancipation Act, but there is plenty of money to be made by those who can buy up the old estates. They show no understanding of the local people or the situation, but even so they don't seem to suffer themselves. Richard Mason, Mr Mason's son, is responsible for Antoinette's marriage to Rochester.

Aunt Cora

Aunt Cora is consistently sensible and sympathetic to both Annette and Antoinette. She distrusts Mr Mason because of his attitude towards the local people, and she disapproves of his behaviour towards Annette. On the night of the fire she keeps everyone calm and arranges for their escape. Later she criticizes Richard Mason when he draws up the marriage arrangements between Antoinette and Mr Rochester. She is angry because she sees that there is no protection for Antoinette; although this was not illegal her relatives could have made sure that she would be provided for after her marriage.

Sandi Cosway
Antoinette's cousin, he appears in all three parts of the novel. In Part One he saves Antoinette from the bullies on the way to school (p. 27), and later on he is referred to as having had a relationship of some kind with Antoinette (pp. 76 and 79). It sounds as if they did love each other, even though there was no possibility of their marrying, both because of their close family relationship and because of the fact that Antoinette was an heiress (p. 120).

Amélie
Young, pretty and ambitious, the servant Amélie does not respect Antoinette, calling her a white cockroach. Rochester uses her to hurt his wife and then sends her away with a little money. She doesn't feel inferior to him, in fact she says she feels sorry for him, but even sorrier for his wife.

Grace Poole
A working-class English woman who is paid well to guard Antoinette in Part Three. She believes that Antoinette is mad but she still feels sorry for her, thinking that Rochester could make sure she is kept warm, better fed and better dressed. Grace has had a hard life. She drinks gin in the evenings, which allows her charge to escape.

Discussion points concerning the characters
None of the characters can be said to be good or bad: most suffer, and some make others suffer too. All are caught in their circumstances. We are not entirely sure even about Antoinette: is she innocent or devious or mad?

Discuss how much the author uses the following narrative devices to explore character: first-person narrative; stream of consciousness; dreams.

Text Summary

(brief description of content Part by Part)

Part One

This is told in Antoinette's voice, and is set in the Jamaica of the mid-1830s. Coulibri, the estate where she grows up, is a beautiful place but, since the death of her father and the Emancipation Act of 1833, it has fallen into decay. Antoinette is ignored by her mother, Annette, who is obsessed with her sick son, Pierre, and by the fact that they are socially excluded by both the black and the better-off white communities. Antoinette becomes increasingly fearful of both the forest and of other people: the forest because it is swallowing up houses and roads in its overwhelming greenness, and the people because they laugh. Even the servants she grew up with have secrets and practise obeah, or magic. Her one friend, Tia, steals her dress and later throws a stone at her. Antoinette's life changes when her mother remarries. They have money and eat English food, but when the house is fired by the local people, Pierre dies; her mother goes mad and dies too. Antoinette is sent away to school. When she leaves at the age of seventeen, she is a wealthy heiress and her fate is sealed.

Part Two

This is set on the island of Dominica, at an estate called Granbois, near the village of Massacre, where Antoinette and Mr Rochester go for their honeymoon. It is told largely in the voice of Mr Rochester (though we are never told his name). Antoinette has lost her own voice on her marriage, except for the sequence when she goes to seek help from her old nurse. She also loses her name when her husband starts to call her Bertha. We see the failure of their marriage from his point of view. He considers himself a victim of the patriarchal system: as a younger son, he needed to find a fortune, and he thinks he has been pressured into marrying a girl of whom he knows nothing. He feels acutely discomfited by the country and by the fact that the girl is at home and he is not. He is unnerved by her pleasure in their love-making, and starts to judge her by the double standard of his society. There are many things he does not understand about the place and the culture, and he gradually lets his fears overcome his reason. He accepts rumours and comes to believe that Antoinette is mad like her mother and brother, and that she is sexually incontinent, though the reader is invited to question who is actually going mad as his language becomes increasingly fractured and fragmented.

By the end of Part Two Antoinette has become a slave. She has lost her happiness, her husband's love, her name, her money and her freedom. She is also about to lose her country and be taken to England.

Part Three
The novel moves to England, to Thornfield Hall, and the narrative continues partly in the words of Grace Poole (a character from the Brontë novel) and partly from inside the mind of Antoinette/Bertha. It concludes with her about to start the fire: 'Now at last I know why I was brought here and what I have to do.'

Critical Responses

For a long time Jean Rhys's fiction was considered limited by the fact that she was a woman and seemed to write only about her own life. However, her first critic, Ford Madox Ford, who did so much to encourage her at the beginning of her career, clearly thought of her as a modernist. For example, in his introduction to her first volume of stories in 1927 he particularly praised her 'singular instinct for form', which he pointed out was 'rare for writers in English and rarer still for English women writers' (Jean Rhys, *The Left Bank and other Stories*, introduced by Ford Madox Ford (London: Jonathan Cape, 1927)).

Reviewers of her first four novels also identified her with the modern school, comparing her with Ernest Hemingway and Katherine Mansfield, even though they were struck as much by her subject matter as by her style. They made such comments as: 'the sordid little story is written with admirable clarity and economy of language' and 'the truth about the grotesque and ugly and contemptible side of life could scarcely be better told than it is told here'(quoted by Rachel Bowlby, in 'The Impasse', in *Still Crazy After All Those Years* (London: Routledge, 1993), p. 34).

The obscurity into which her work fell until the late 1950s may have been caused both by her subject matter and by her Bohemian lifestyle. For example, she wrote about girls drifting into prostitution and having abortions, which was quite shocking at the time. As a young woman she moved around a lot, living in London, Paris and Vienna. She had affairs and three husbands, two of whom spent time in prison. She spent much of her life in poverty and in later life suffered from alcoholism. Even after the publication of

Wide Sargasso Sea in 1966, when critics began to treat her novels more seriously, she was angered by their tendency to treat her not as a writer but as a woman writer, and one who wrote only about passive female victims. As Helen Carr puts it, the 'anger against injustice and hypocrisy behind Rhys's "terrific – almost lurid! – passion for stating the case of the underdog" disappears from view' (Helen Carr, *Jean Rhys* (Plymouth: Northcote House, 1996), p. 7).

Another possible reason why she was not considered seriously by her contemporaries was because it was felt that she wrote too much about herself, and there was a certain amount of snobbery about the kind of writer she was and the life she led. Typically, her novels described the struggles of young women trying to find themselves and to find the means of supporting themselves. Instead of providing a fashionably happy ending, she described the difficulties they faced as, by society's standards, they all failed.

Judith Kegan Gardiner has pointed out that

when a writer like Joyce or Eliot writes about an alienated man estranged from himself, [such a figure] is read as a portrait of the diminished possibilities of human existence in modern society. When Rhys writes about an alienated woman estranged from herself, critics applaud her perceptive but narrow depiction of female experience and tend to narrow her vision even further by labelling it both pathological and autobiographical ('Good Morning, Midnight: Good Night, Modernism', *Boundary 2*, 11 (1982–3), p. 242).

Likewise her own Bohemian lifestyle was described by critics as drifting and insecure. Critics have tended to forget to point out that she had had high ambitions for a career on the stage but was forced to leave drama college when her father died. Even when she was considered positively in the 1970s and beyond, Helen Carr points out that 'it was very much as a feeling not a thinking writer', almost as an 'ill-educated genius', even though her most famous book is clearly based on another one, and her books are full of literary references (*Jean Rhys*, p. 7).

Jean Rhys published four novels and a book of short stories between 1927 and 1939, including *Quartet* (based on her relationship with Ford), and *Voyage in the Dark* (which also has a heroine who grew up in the Caribbean). She then seemed to disappear. In 1949 Selma Vaz Dias advertised for news of her in the *New Statesman* because she wanted to adapt *Good Morning, Midnight* for BBC Radio. The BBC thought she might be dead, and she was even referred to as 'the late Jean Rhys' in an article by Francis Wyndham. In 1949 she said in a letter that when she contacted the BBC she felt like an impostor pretending to be herself, or indeed like one of the zombies or revenants she writes about. *Wide Sargasso Sea* finally made her name on its publication in 1966. It was immediately successful, winning the Royal Society of Literature Award and the W. II. Smith Award, and has grown in popularity ever since.

This is partly because *Wide Sargasso Sea* anticipates so many late twentieth-century preoccupations: with relationships, with questions of place and belonging, with spaces between cultures, and with fiction from the margins, whether from women or the former empire. It has become a key novel for the discussion of almost every literary theory and term, including feminism, gothic, postcolonialism and intertextuality. Critics have argued over whether it is possible to describe *Wide Sargasso Sea* as a modernist, or a postmodernist, or a feminist, or a post-colonial novel. Or is it all or none of these?

The first critics to get away from the myths and stereotypes based on preconceptions of Jean Rhys's life were critics from the Caribbean. In 1968 Wally Look Lai started the discussion with an essay called 'The Road to Thornfield Hall: An Analysis of *Wide Sargasso Sea*' (London: New Beacon Books, 1968). In 1971 Kenneth Ramchand saw in *Wide Sargasso Sea* the 'alienation within alienation' and the 'terrified consciousness' of the dispossessed colonizer (*The West Indian Novel and Its Background* (London: Faber and Faber, 1970), pp. 225, 231). V. S. Naipaul in 1972 was one of the first to suggest that all her writing should be understood in the light of her colonial origins (see 'Without a Dog's Chance', reprinted in *Critical Perspectives on Jean Rhys*, ed. P. Frickey (Washington: Three Continent Press, 1990), p. 54). In 1974 John Hearne described Rhys with Wilson Harris as 'guerrillas, not outsiders', in his essay 'The Wide Sargasso Sea: a West Indian Reflection' (*Cornhill Magazine*, 1080, (Summer 1974)).

Edward Said's *Orientalism* (New York: Vintage, 1979) pointed out how the European imperial powers saw their colonial subjects as representing what they found most fearful (the dark, the irrational, the other). Said stressed the importance of cultural texts like *Wide Sargasso Sea* 'in the great game of colony and empire, of race and its deployment' (Padmini Mongia, *Contemporary Postcolonial Theory* (London: Arnold, 1997), p. 4). Although more recently some critics, such as Gayatri Spivak (1985), Molly Hite (1989) and Veronica Gregg (1995), have found Jean Rhys's portrayals of the West Indies and race unacceptable, others such as Elaine Savory consider that she was in many ways ahead of her time in her willingness to deal with race (*Jean Rhys* (Cambridge University Press, 1998), p. 135).

As Judie Newman pointed out in 1995, where Charlotte Brontë made Bertha and Jane opposites in a kind of war of the women, Rhys reverses these tactics. She gives Bertha a similar childhood to Jane's. The only real difference is their position, one on the edge of the empire, the other at its centre. Antoinette's personal history is firmly politicized. She is the daughter of former slave-owners in post-Emancipation Jamaica, and so is automatically hated by both the black and the mixed-race populations, as well as by the wealthier whites. Antoinette is also rejected by her mother, leading to lack of self-confidence, while the weak mother–child bond reflects the relationship of mother country–child colony. She represents only wealth to Mr Rochester, who is incapable of regarding her as an equal. He becomes increasingly distanced from her, coming to the conclusion that she must be mad, and taking away her freedom. There are of course clear political parallels.

By the mid-1990s, therefore, Judie Newman assumed that *Wide Sargasso Sea* could be read as both a feminist and a post-colonial text. However, in the early 1970s critics were not sure whether Jean Rhys was a feminist writer. The first full-length book on Rhys's work, by Louis James in 1978, was criticized for being too feminist an interpretation of her work. Critics felt that feminist writers should present only positive female images, whereas Rhys's heroines were all passive and all failed to achieve what they wanted in life, or even to find out what that was.

However, some key books in the 1970s, such as those by Ellen Moers and Elaine Showalter, were encouraging the promotion of the tradition of writing by women, particularly forgotten or marginalized women writers. A key critical book was *The Madwoman in the Attic: the woman writer and the nineteenth-century literary imagination* by Sandra M. Gilbert and Susan Gubar (New Haven and London: Yale University Press, 1979), which took the image of the encounter between Jane Eyre and Bertha Mason as the central confrontation of the book, and indeed of the whole tradition of women's writing: 'an encounter . . . with her own imprisoned "hunger, rebellion and rage", a secret dialogue of self and soul on whose outcome . . . the novel's plot, Rochester's fate, and Jane's coming-of-age all depend' (p. 339).

They investigated the association between women and madness, and found that it had layers of meanings. There were social and psychological reasons why women might go, or be considered, 'mad': women led restricted lives, their ambitions were often considered 'mad'. Their lives were in the hands of their husbands and male relatives. They could be locked up, divorced and deprived of their children and money if they were diagnosed 'mad'. But in *Jane Eyre* the mad woman is clearly part of Jane herself, and so of the author, the wild, untamed, untameable part.

As Gilbert and Gubar say in their introduction, they discovered in the early 1970s:

a distinctively female literary tradition, a tradition that had been approached and appreciated by many women readers and writers but which no one had yet defined in its entirety. Images of enclosure and escape, fantasies in which maddened doubles functioned as asocial surrogates for docile selves, metaphors of physical discomfort manifested in frozen landscapes and fiery interiors – such patterns recurred throughout this tradition, along with obsessive depictions of diseases like anorexia, agoraphobia and claustrophobia (p. xi).

Enclosed in the architecture of an overwhelmingly male-dominated society, these literary women were also, inevitably, trapped in the specifically literary constructs of what Gertrude Stein was to call 'patriarchal poetry'. For not only might a nineteenth-century woman writer have to inhabit ancestral mansions owned and built by men, she was also constricted and restricted by the literary world that male writers had created. Just as the discontented ex-slaves set fire to Coulibri, so Antoinette/Bertha sets fire to Thornfield Hall, the house in which she finds herself imprisoned by her husband.

Feminism like post-colonialism is constructed around binaries, such as masculine/feminine, activity/passivity, sun/moon, culture/nature, day/night, reason/madness. In *Jane Eyre*, the heroine must meet and overcome oppression, starvation, madness and coldness, in order to attain the goal of mature freedom. Jane achieves this goal but Antoinette does not. On the other hand, Jane's is a limited goal, that of marriage, whereas Antoinette goes beyond this. As Graham Allen points out, nineteenth-century novels end in either marriage or death for women; that is, success or failure. Women do not have such extensive quests as men. Twentieth-century novels go beyond the marriage and the couple. In *Jane Eyre* the heroine can marry only because Bertha/Antoinette fails as a wife. The ideal Victorian wife depends on the failure of the 'dangerous "other" who haunts the margins of Brontë's novel' (Graham Allen, *Intertextuality* (London: Routledge, 2000), p. 150). But of course in *Wide Sargasso Sea* Bertha/Antoinette is triply 'other': she is mad, female and a mulatto colonial subject. Rhys ends the book by taking us to this heart of 'otherness': 'It was red and all my life was in it' (*WSS*, p. 123).

In patriarchy, women are always what men are not; but this is too simple to explain the difference between Charlotte Brontë in the nineteenth century and Jean Rhys in the twentieth century. By the time of *Wide Sargasso Sea* the mad woman is no longer the 'other' as in Brontë but the 'self': Antoinette tells the story. The one from the margins, the unvoiced, the disempowered, becomes the heroine and dies by fire. The key relationship here is between two women writers, not between male and female writers. Here the intertextual relationship explores both gender and post-colonial politics.

Increasingly critics have described *Wide Sargasso Sea* as being all these things, and more. For example, some say it is more than modernist. The fact that it evades closure makes it postmodernist. We assume that the ending will be the same as in *Jane Eyre*, but it does not have to be. *Wide Sargasso Sea* is a feminist text in that it describes what it is like to be a woman in a male-dominated society, but the novel is also about what it is like to come from a colony in an imperial society. Above all, *Wide Sargasso Sea* is about what it means to be a writer, 'writing back' from the margins. Its intertextual relationship with *Jane Eyre* draws all these different interpretations together.

As Helen Carr says, Jean Rhys's position as 'migrant, marginal, homeless, never (as she says in *Quartet*) "quite of the fold", made it possible for her to write novels which both went to the heart of the prejudices, exclusions and paranoia of the period in which she wrote, and as well explore a dimension of modernist, even post-modernist consciousness that perhaps only appears elsewhere before the Second World War in Kafka's work' (*Jean Rhys*, p. xiv).

Her fiction, dealing as it does with those who belong nowhere, between cultures, between histories, describes an existence which is now commonplace. It is, of course, a threat to those who like literature, and life, to be neatly compartmentalized (just as Mr Rochester, disliking the female world of the honeymoon island, decides that Antoinette is mad and sexually incontinent, makes her a prisoner, puts himself in control, and takes her back to England).

Critics have discussed why Jean Rhys introduces the rather stereotypical issues of magic, voodoo, obeah. One explanation is that they are all ways in which people try to take control of their lives and those of other people. In the same way, Jean Rhys takes control of an English canonical novel, and makes it live again. The Brontë text becomes a ghost and haunts *Wide Sargasso Sea*. Likewise, Jean Rhys makes Mr Rochester become blind as the result of Christophine's curse. The theme of magic introduces many themes: What is reality? What is the role of reason or justice? Can there be any possibility of two worlds understanding each other?

Judie Newman interprets the end of the novel as being the opposite of Charlotte Brontë's. In Christian myth, fire and hellfire go together, a fit punishment for those who are damned already. But she points out that the Arawak people, the first inhabitants of Dominica, had a myth about a tree of life which, though burning, would drive those who took refuge in it up into the sky to become stars. So when Antoinette looks out from the battlements of Thornfield Hall, she sees images from her past: 'It was red and all my life was in it. I saw the grandfather clock and Aunt Cora's patchwork, all colours, I saw the orchids and the stephanotis and the jasmine and the tree of life in flames' (p. 123). This takes us back to the beginning of the novel, to her childhood and to the garden that she loved so much. But it also gives a more positive reading to the text when on the final page she says: 'The wind caught my hair and it streamed out like wings. It might bear me up, I thought'. The presence of magic, of references to other cultures and other languages in the novel alerts us to the fact that there might be other readings than Brontë's.

'I often wonder who I am and where is my country and where do I belong and why was I ever born at all,' says Antoinette (p. 63). Jean Rhys too was preoccupied with the precariousness of identity. Whether this came from her own experience as a woman, as a colonial, from her own ambiguous status in society or her experience as a writer at a time when all certainties had gone, the issue of identity affects us all. Each reader will come to the text with different viewpoints and will find different things in it. As Helen Carr says, 'Jean Rhys cannot be considered exclusively as a Caribbean writer, or as a woman writer, a novelist of the demi-monde, or as a modernist. She is all of those, but being all of those, none fit her as unproblematic labels' (*Jean Rhys*, p. xiv).

Suggestions for Further Reading

Wide Sargasso Sea, ed. Angela Smith (Harmondsworth: Penguin, 1997) – this edition has a useful introduction, and also reprints Francis Wyndham's introduction to the first edition.

Wide Sargasso Sea: Backgrounds, Criticism (Norton Critical Edition), ed. Judith Raiskin (Norton, 1998) – useful edition with selection of letters, key articles and relevant passages from *Jane Eyre*.

Jean Rhys, Helen Carr (Plymouth: Northcote House, 1996) – clear, short introduction to the complete work of Jean Rhys.

The Ballistic Bard, Judie Newman (London: Arnold, 1995) – Chapter 2 is a useful essay entitled 'I walked with a zombie'. This was the title of a film made in 1943 by Val Lewton, and described by him as 'Jane Eyre in the tropics'. It is likely that Jean Rhys saw this film.

Jean Rhys, Sylvie Maurel (London: Macmillan, 1998) – another short book covering all Jean Rhys's novels.

Voyage in the Dark, Jean Rhys (Harmondsworth: Penguin, 1969) – another novel by Rhys with a heroine from the West Indies.

Jean Rhys Revisited, Alexis Lykiard (Exeter: Stride, 2000) – a recent memoir which includes interesting material about the later life of Jean Rhys, and the writing of *Wide Sargasso Sea*.

Intertextuality, Graham Allen (London: Routledge, 2000) – an introduction to intertextuality, with some references to Jean Rhys.

Literature, Peter Widdowson (London: Routledge, 1999) – a useful introduction to studying literature, with a chapter on novels which 'write back' to classic texts.

Examples of other novels which 'write back':

Foe, J. M. Coetzee (Harmondsworth: Penguin, 1987), to *Robinson Crusoe*.

Estella: Her Expectations, by Sue Roe (Brighton: Harvester, 1982), to *Great Expectations*.

Indigo or, Mapping the Waters, by Marina Warner (London: Chatto & Windus, 1992), to *The Tempest*.

A Thousand Acres by Jane Smiley (London: Flamingo/Harper Collins, 1991), to *King Lear*.

Contemporary Postcolonial Theory, ed. Padmini Mongia (London: Arnold, 1997) – for those who wish to read more about post-colonial theory.

The Arnold Anthology of Post-Colonial Literatures in English, ed. John Thieme (London: Arnold, 1996) – for those who wish to read more post-colonial literature.

Critical Theory & Practice: A Coursebook, Keith Green and Jill LeBihan (London: Routledge, 1996) – a general introduction to all the major theories, with some references to Jean Rhys.

The Madwoman in the Attic, Sandra M. Gilbert and Susan Gubar (London: Yale University Press, 1979) – the key text on the history of women's writing, focusing on the figure of Bertha Mason, as the madwoman in the attic.

Audio Extracts 🎧

PART ONE

pp. 3.1–7.16
pp. 11.23–12.16
pp. 18.23–23.24

PART TWO

pp. 54.15–55.4
pp. 56.31–60.24
pp. 105.16–108.23
pp. 112.28–113.20

PART THREE

pp. 115.16–123.31.

Total = approx. 73 minutes

READ MORE IN PENGUIN

In every corner of the world, on every subject under the sun, Penguin represents quality and variety – the very best in publishing today.

For complete information about books available from Penguin – including Puffins, Penguin Classics and Arkana – and how to order them, write to us at the appropriate address below. Please note that for copyright reasons the selection of books varies from country to country.

In the United Kingdom: Please write to *Dept. EP, Penguin Books Ltd, Bath Road, Harmondsworth, West Drayton, Middlesex UB7 0DA*

In the United States: Please write to *Consumer Sales, Penguin Putnam Inc., P.O. Box 12289 Dept. B, Newark, New Jersey 07101-5289.* VISA and MasterCard holders call 1-800-788-6262 to order Penguin titles

In Canada: Please write to *Penguin Books Canada Ltd, 10 Alcorn Avenue, Suite 300, Toronto, Ontario M4V 3B2*

In Australia: Please write to *Penguin Books Australia Ltd, P.O. Box 257, Ringwood, Victoria 3134*

In New Zealand: Please write to *Penguin Books (NZ) Ltd, Private Bag 102902, North Shore Mail Centre, Auckland 10*

In India: Please write to *Penguin Books India Pvt Ltd, 11 Community Centre, Panchsheel Park, New Delhi 110017*

In the Netherlands: Please write to *Penguin Books Netherlands bv, Postbus 3507, NL-1001 AH Amsterdam*

In Germany: Please write to *Penguin Books Deutschland GmbH, Metzlerstrasse 26, 60594 Frankfurt am Main*

In Spain: Please write to *Penguin Books S. A., Bravo Murillo 19, 1° B, 28015 Madrid*

In Italy: Please write to *Penguin Italia s.r.l., Via Benedetto Croce 2, 20094 Corsico, Milano*

In France: Please write to *Penguin France, Le Carré Wilson, 62 rue Benjamin Baillaud, 31500 Toulouse*

In Japan: Please write to *Penguin Books Japan Ltd, Kaneko Building, 2-3-25 Koraku, Bunkyo-Ku, Tokyo 112*

In South Africa: Please write to *Penguin Books South Africa (Pty) Ltd, Private Bag X14, Parkview, 2122 Johannesburg*

PENGUIN STUDENT EDITIONS

Series Editors: Ronald Carter and John McRae

Penguin Student Editions have been specifically designed for readers who are studying a text in detail. They include a helpful introduction and explanatory notes, character sketches, a text summary, a chronology, language notes, a selection of questions and topics for discussion and analysis, as well as suggestions for further reading.

Also published: